Unexpected Crossroads

A REAL HOOD ROMANCE

Blossom Carter

ISBN: 1532890990

ISBN 13: 9781532890994

Acknowledgments

Before I thank anyone, I want to take the time to thank God for all he has done for me over the years. Not even three years ago, I was down at rock bottom, fighting depression. Never in a million years would I have thought that I'd be where I am today. After all of the bullshit that life threw my way, I owe my life and my soul to God. He came into my life and showed me that I could be happy again and that I should never lose sight of faith. Even when things seem bad, you have to remain focused and keep your faith. Without you, I'm nothing. I lost everything because I allowed anger to keep me from you. Now look at me. I'm beyond blessed, and I owe it all to you. I've seen what life can be like without you, and believe me—I wouldn't wish that life on anyone. *Unexpected Crossroads* has been the most challenging, fun, exhausting project I've ever worked on. There were so many times when I wanted to quit, but you wouldn't let me. You kept reminding me that there was still work to be done. Every day this book was in my heart and on my mind. I enjoy writing, and I thank you for the bomb gift that you've given me. I couldn't ask for a better King to serve. You're the light of my heart and my world, and I'm so thankful for the blood of Jesus. Thank you, God—I love you. *Unexpected Crossroads* couldn't have happened without you.

Next I would like to thank my two favorite cousins, Shalia and India, for being the first two people to read *Unexpected Crossroads* and for giving me their honest opinions and helping me through this journey. You two stayed on my ass about this book and couldn't wait to read it. You two kept me motivated and always had something positive to say when I needed to hear it the most. I really appreciate all of the love and support from you guys. I love y'all—I can't stress that enough. Thank you for everything. This is just the beginning—we're going to ride this wave till the end. I want to thank my cousin Ria for doing my photo shoot and for supporting me through this journey. You know I love you, fam. Shit's always been real and solid between us. To those who read *Unexpected Crossroads*, if you're ever in Indianapolis, Indiana, and need your hair slayed for the Gods, come get a dose of your new addiction, and let Weaves_by_ria slay your hair. I would also like to thank my best friend, Tre Tre. You're a pain in my ass, but, hey, I love you anyway—even though you think I'm downright mean and crazy. I want to take the time to thank you for being a great friend and for supporting me through it all. You will forever have a place in my heart. I know I don't tell you this much, but I love you, my nigga, and nothing will ever change that.

Thank you, Mommy, for giving me life and for telling me to go out and chase my dreams. I admire you. You have always been a hustler. I've never met a woman who's as strong as you. You birthed a queen, and I'm grateful to have you as my mother. Thank you, Daddy, for believing in me and for telling me that "the only thing that comes to a sleeper is a dream." That shit stuck with me, and now I barely sleep. You showed me that there's no price on your dreams and that it takes money to make money. I love you, Daddy. I've never told you this, but I admire you as well. I watched you go from driving semitrucks for other people to owning your own trucking company, and I'm very proud of you. I know I'm a pain in your ass, but I love you, Daddy, and I couldn't ask for a better man to be my father.

I want to give a shout-out to my homey Big Mike, who reached out to me and showed me the importance of patience when I didn't have any. I like things done my way and on my time, but you opened my eyes. I know you felt that I wasn't listening, because I hate being told what to do, but I was, and I took in a lot of the things that you said. I appreciate you, and I can't wait to you show the world all of the gifts that God has blessed you with. I'm rooting for you, my nigga, and I'll see you at the top, because that's the only place to go. I also want to give a shout-out to my big cousin Twan, who I consider a brother, not a cousin. Thank you, fam, for just motivating me. I've been watching you for years, and I swear that I've never met a man who can hustle like you can. Thank you for all of the support and all of the real talks we had about life, God, and much more. I love you, fam, and I can't wait for the world to hear you. their not ready for you—for real, though.

I saved the best for last. Thank you, Anthony J. Lloyd, my twin. If it hadn't been for your death, I wouldn't be half the woman I am today. Every time I think about giving up, I hear your voice say, "E Keep pushing, and pick ya head up." You don't know how down I was when you left, but now I'm living every day for you. I'm so pissed off that you're not here, but I know that you're watching over me and that God doesn't make mistakes. You don't know how happy I was when you came to me in a dream and told me how proud you were of me for writing this book. I swear, I cried like a baby when I woke up. Never in a million years would I have thought that you wouldn't be here with me today to watch me live out my dreams. But truth be told, it wasn't until you passed away that I learned that I love to write. It was the only thing that made me happy at that time. It's my getaway from the hurt I carry every day. There aren't enough words or emotions to explain the way I feel and the love I have for you. I know you'll be waiting for me at the crossroads to walk me through them gates, but until then, I'll be missing you, my twin. GFM till I die. God, family, money—nothing comes before, between, or after.

I dedicate this book to my brother—my twin, Anthony J. Lloyd (February 8, 1994–September 24, 2013). I love you, twin. In this world or the next, you shall forever be a part of me.

Memory Lane (Cinnamon)

"My old bitches, they're maniacs, and my new bitches, they're psychos, and one day they'll both get along. What can I say? I got high hopes," I said, rapping along to Don Trip's "Still in the Trap" as I cleaned my two-bedroom condo. I can honestly say that I could relate to a lot of the shit in the song. You see, my mind-set was a lot different from most bitches'. I wasn't your typical girl who wanted to be in love or who was going to chase after a nigga at that. I really didn't give two fucks about a nigga. I'd been that way ever since I could remember. I'd always had a nonchalant attitude toward men—until my ex came along.

Let's just say that one bad experience with love left me on some fuck-a-nigga shit. I was in a relationship for two years, and everything was a lie. I treated him like a king, instead of like the peasant that I knew he was. That nigga didn't want for shit. I'm a freak at heart—that comes natural to me—and he had anything and everything that a man could have asked for in a woman, and he still cheated. That just goes to show you that no matter how much you love a nigga, how long you ride with him, or how much of a freak you are, a nigga is going to do whatever he wants, no matter what. From that day on, I vowed to never let another nigga get over on me or to even get comfortable, for that matter. My phone began to ring, and I was happy because I was starting to get pissed all over again just thinking about it.

"Hello," I said with a little attitude.

"Well, damn. Who pissed in your cheerios this morning?" my cousin Chyna asked me.

"My bad, girl. I was just thinking about some old shit, and it threw me off. Where the hell are you hos at? Y'all were supposed to be here an hour ago."

"I know. Blame Stonie. You know it takes that bitch an hour just to pick out a damn shirt." I could hear Stonie in the background, talking shit as usual. I didn't know why she was, because she knew that she was the slow one out of the group. I wouldn't be surprised if she were late to her own damn funeral.

"How far are y'all for real, Chyna?"

"We'll be there in an hour," she said, but I hung up the phone before she could get another word out. I knew how they were—they were probably just leaving Indianapolis. Chyna and Stonie are my cousins, and we're all like best friends. Chyna is the one with the brains. She's very smart—a little too smart, if you ask me—and crazy as hell with a dark side that makes me wonder if she's ever killed anyone before, with the kind of thoughts that she has. Stonie is the hustler in the group: she does hair, nails, and makeup, and she can sing her ass off. We call her "Stonie" because she's always as high as a kite. I missed being around my cousins and just being able to pull up on them when I didn't have anything else better to do.

I'd moved to Chicago about a year, after the breakup with my ex. I'd needed a new start—something like a getaway, you could say. As I walked to the back of my condo and to my room, I thought about how far

I'd come in the last year or so. Once I was in my room, I reached into my nightstand and grabbed a jar of weed. I had a little time to spare before they got to my house, and I needed a blunt. Those bitches were getting on my nerves, and they weren't even in town yet. Once I had my Swisher broken down, I began to look through my text messages. I had a few un- read messages from some niggas I'd given my number to a while back. I didn't care about handing my number out, because I could look at my phone and simply not answer texts or calls. I don't do that block-list shit. I'll watch the phone ring and not answer it. Once you text me back to back, I'll open up your text to let you know that I read it and still not reply. I hate a worrisome-ass nigga. Just be yourself. Either I'm gonna fuck with you, or I'm not. I hate the niggas who try to sell dreams. Whatever hap- pened to keeping it real? "I guess I'm asking for too much," I thought to myself as I rolled my blunt.

Once I had rolled and lit my blunt, I inhaled the weed, threw my head back, and let out the smoke. "Yes, I needed that," I said out loud to my- self. After checking my text messages, I walked over to my walk-in closet. I needed to get dressed before they got there and started talking shit. As I began to look through my closet for something to wear, I decided on a money-green loose sweater dress with some thigh-high red-burgundy boots. It was the beginning of April, and it wasn't hot or cold. The weath- er was just right—a little windy, but that was all. I threw what I planned on wearing for the day and a matching bra-and-pantie set on my bed. I walked over to the bathroom and started the shower while I put out the rest of my blunt. Hell, I was already higher than a giraffe's pussy, and I still had a half of a blunt left.

I took my clothes off and hopped into the shower, letting the water hit my face and run down my body. Honestly, I had a lot on my mind, and being sexually frustrated didn't help. It had been eight months since the last time I'd had sex, and I was tired of getting myself off, so that was out of the question. Getting some dick wasn't the hard part. Finding someone who I actually liked was the problem. I snapped out of my thoughts and grabbed my kai body wash and handled my business. Thirty minutes later I got out of the shower, dried off, put lotion on, and got dressed. I unwrapped my twenty-two-inch brazilin weave, letting it fall down my back. I applied some eyeliner and mascara. I've never been big on makeup. I don't feel that I need it, and I want to look the same in the morning when I wake up and at night. Besides, true beauty comes from within.

After putting on my burgundy Mac lipstick, I gave myself an over-all look. I must say that I looked good. I'm five foot seven with brown skin, the deepest dimples, and a slim-thick body. I call myself "slim thick" because I'm not thick or little—my size is just right, and my ass was sitting just right in that dress, even though it was baggy. For twenty-two, I was doing damn good. I had a great-paying job that I loved and a brand-new 2016 BMW, and my condo was laid out from front to back. A nigga couldn't have done shit for me that I couldn't have done for myself. "I don't have shit for a nigga but a hard time," I thought to myself as I glanced over at the clock and shook my head.

An hour had passed, and they weren't there yet. As soon as I grabbed my blunt from earlier and lit it, I heard a knock on my front door. I knew it had to be them, because nobody other than family knew where I laid my head. I made sure to walk extra slow to the front door—I even thought about finishing my blunt before opening the door. When I opened the door, I blew smoke right in Chyna's face.

"You're truly a rude-ass bitch," Chyna said.

"And you hos are truly late, so what's the difference?"

They just pushed their way past me and came right in.

Chyna

During the whole ride from Indianapolis to Chicago, I was in a daze and just in my own world. I needed this trip to clear my mind. I had an on-again-off-again relationship with my man. It was getting to the point that I no longer wanted to be with him. I didn't understand why it was so hard to leave. Don't get me wrong—I still loved him, but what real woman would want to put up with a cheating, broke-ass nigga? It wasn't about the money with me. But how could he be broke and still think that he could try to shit on me? I was at a point where I was just fed up and wanted out of my relationship, but that was easier said than done. After Stonie and I pulled up to Cinnamon's house, we gathered our bags and knocked on the door for what seemed like forever.

"I know she's in there," Stonie said. She really had us sitting out there for a good minute with those heavy-ass bags in our hands. I was about to knock harder, but she opened the door and blew smoke right in my face. My cousin is the true definition of an asshole, top flight, to be exact. I didn't pay her any mind. We just pushed past her and walked up the stairs.

"Is that any way to treat your guests?" Stonie asked while walking over to the couch to sit down.

"Girl, please. You bitches are not guests, because if you were, you'd be at a hotel, not my damn house," Cinnamon said. I grabbed an already-rolled blunt and lit it. My cousin Cinnamon can seem like a real bitch at times, but she has a big heart. She's just a little too overly blunt, and she doesn't have a problem speaking her mind—nor does she feel bad when she says what she has to say.

"So what are the plans now that we're here?"

"I could use a shopping spree." Cinnamon and I both looked over at Stonie because every day is a shopping spree for her—her house is like a minimall.

5

"You know you're the last person who should be talking about a shopping spree."

She just stuck her middle finger up at me and mouthed the words "fuck you" while grabbing the blunt that I was passing to her. Cinnamon walked to the kitchen and brought back three shot glasses and a bottle of Patron.

"Since y'all are here, let's take a couple of shots before we hit these Chicago streets." It wasn't even five in the evening yet, and we were already turned up. That's what I love about my cousins—you can always have a good time with them. We sat for the next hour, talking, taking shots, and passing the blunt—that is, until my phone began to rang. It was nobody other than James. I immediately got irritated because every conversation we had ended with an argument, so I know this one wont be different.

"Hello," I said, a bit nonchalantly. I'd known that it would only be a matter of time before he called with his bullshit. I wasn't trying to sound like I didn't want to talk, but I knew him and knew that an argument was right around the corner.

"I know you made it to Chicago, so why haven't I heard from you?"

I really had to brace myself. That question alone had me wanting to say that if he wanted to try to control someone, he should go have some damn kids. That shit wasn't going to fly with me. It took everything in me to answer the question without getting smart. The last thing I needed was for Stonie or Cinnamon to get on my case—they already hated his guts.

"We really just got here not even an hour ago. I haven't had time to even unpack, let alone to call you and tell you that I made it."

"Yeah, all right, Chyna. We'll see," he said, and then he hung up. I started to call him back to tell him how I felt about him, but that was what he wanted me to do, so I didn't do it. I planned on enjoying myself that weekend. Before I could even get all of the way off the phone, Cinnamon was on my head like a fitted cap.

"I don't know how you put up with his bum ass. I'm not tryin' to be mean, but what is it that you see in him?"

"Cinnamon, don't start, please."

"I'm not starting shit. I'm just saying that that's one insecure-ass nigga you're dealing with."

"Yeah, like, bitch, for real. I want to know why you're still fucking with this nigga too. He doesn't have shit, and he's always cheating on you. Why the hell are you letting a broke-ass nigga dog you? I mean, you shouldn't let any man treat you like shit, but a broke nigga has no room to be doing shit other than what's right."

I let out a deep breath and threw my head back. "Great," I thought. "Now I have both Cinnamon and Stonie on my case." I grabbed the bottle of Patron, took another shot, and started thinking to myself for a few minutes.

"Honestly, y'all, don't laugh, but I think it's his dick game—seriously." Cinnamon burst out laughing. I couldn't even finish what I had to say.

"So basically, what you're telling us is that you went 'dick dumb.'"

As much as I wanted to cuss her out, I couldn't do anything but laugh. She's the only person I know who could come up with some shit like that to say.

"I'm done with you hos for today."

"Good, because I'm done talking about this. Period," Stonie said.

"Let's go eat or go shopping. We didn't drive all the way here to talk about that nigga."

Once that had been said, no more than fifteen minutes later, we were up and out of the house, ready to hit the streets of Chicago.

Chapter Two

(Malik)
The Street Is Mine

"Shut the fuck up, and stop all that damn crying. You weren't crying when you were stealing our shit, now were you?" my little brother, Markese, yelled as I walked through the chop shop. I had to make this quick—I had shit to do. When I walked into the room, they already had B tied down to a chair, and from the look of things, he had been getting his ass beat for breakfast, lunch, and dinner. I dapped my cousin Dominique, who was sitting off to the side and smoking a blunt without a care in the world. He had seen worse and done much worse to people, so this didn't faze him. If anything, he was bored. I walked over to where they had B tied up and gave Markese some dap. B looked up at me with swollen eyes, and it looked like his jaw was broken, based on the way it was hanging and the blood that was running out of his mouth. I had no sympathy for him at all. When I looked at the floor, I saw teeth everywhere—not two or three but a mouthful of teeth. These niggas had left him toothless with nothing but gums.

I'm not one to do no talking, especially when it comes to my money. A hundred grand wasn't shit to me—I wiped my ass with that. It was the fact that he'd stolen it from me. At the end of the day, it was the principle of it. I'd worked hard to get where I was. Even if he'd stolen five dollars, what was mine was mine. B had no reason to steal from me. All of the niggas who worked for me were paid with big houses and a hell of ice, so there weren't any excuses. A money-hungry nigga will never make it in this world, and the love of money was why this pussy nigga wont see tomorrow or his kids again. I couldn't have cared less about what he had to say, if he could even talk at all. I wasted no time and grabbed the .40-caliber Glock. I gave him two to the head and put him to sleep for good.

I looked over to Markese, who was then rolling a blunt. "Call the clean-up crew. This shit needs to be cleaned up ASAP." There were teeth, bloodstains, and brains all over the floor and walls. I walked over to Dominique, sat next to him, put my head in my hands, and let out a deep breath.

"You coo', fam? Everything straight?" Dominique asked me.

"Yeah, I'm straight."

I was just thinking about how far we'd come. Not even five years ago, I'd still been hustling on the block, trying to take care of my family. I'd gotten tired of seeing my mother struggle to take care of my brother, my baby sister, and me all by herself because my bitch-ass father had walked out on her when I was eight. He'd left her to take care of three kids by herself, and at the age of fourteen, I began selling weed. That was the only way I could make any money at my age. That shit was easy—it was like I'd been born to hustle. The only reason I went to school was because more than half of my clientele was there. By the age of sixteen, I "caught" my first body—he was some nigga I'd been serving awhile. He tried to rob me of everything I had, but I was a little nigga with a heart of a lion. Before any nigga could take from me, we had to shoot it out.

Even at the age of sixteen, I wasn't a punk. Killing never fazed me after that night. Shortly after I "bagged" my first nigga, word got around fast that I wasn't to be fucked with. I stayed in the streets throughout my teenage years. By the time I was twenty, my name rang bells on every side of Chicago. All of the OGs knew me and had respect for me.

I'm cut differently than a lot of niggas are. I believe in loyalty, trust, and respect. That shit is built into me. If you don't show those three qualities, you're better off dead, in my opinion. When I turned twenty-one, I found my first plug, and I've been on ever since then. Markese, Dominique, and I had then started moving bricks of cocaine in and out of the city. I felt that if I was gonna risk my freedom, it wouldn't be over no pounds of weed. I told myself that I was gonna do it big, and that's just what I did. I'd made more money than I knew what to do with, and I'd seen enough money to last me three lifetimes. I had most of the Chicago police force on my payroll. I hated the pigs, but if I wanted to keep my black ass out of jail, I had to pay them dirty muthafuckas.

I'm nothing like the kingpins you hear about. I don't look down on anyone, and I don't treat others as if I'm better than they are. All I ask is that they don't cross me. If they don't, everything will run smoothly. Even though I started this operation, I wouldn't be where I am today without my brothers' help. Dominique may be my cousin, but in my eyes, he's my brother. My mother took him in after his mother was murdered. We grew up in the same household, fought, and made up like brothers would have. What was mine was theirs, and this is our city, and it would be a cold day in hell before anyone could think about coming along and taking it from me. I snapped out of my thoughts when I heard voices and footsteps in the room.

"Damn, it's about time that you niggas showed up." I stood up and dapped both Brandon and Corey. If you wanted a body gone, never to be seen again, they were the two white muthafuckas you would want to hire to get the job done. Those two were the craziest niggas I'd ever come across. They didn't give any fucks—they were about action. They'd kill your grandma for the right price with no questions asked.

"My bad, fam. This nigga was knee-deep in some pussy when we got the call," Corey said. I couldn't do anything but shake my head.

"Y'all niggas know what to do to that nigga over there. Try to make it quick." I looked over at Dominique, and it looked like he had a lot on his mind. I knew that look. Ever since Dominique's mother had been killed, he hadn't been the same. The nigga was fucked up in the head to the point of no return. He was probably about to go "body" a nigga or two—you never knew with him.

"Aye, I'm out of here, fam. I'll catch up with you later." He nodded his head and finished smoking his blunt as I walked out of the chop shop. I spotted Markese standing next to his Porsche, smoking a blunt. He walked over to where my 2016 Rolls-Royce was parked and handed me the blunt.

"What're you about to get into, fam?" I asked him.

"Shit, after they clean up and go, I'm gonna swing by the traps to make sure that everything's straight for tomorrow's shipment. After that I'm gonna meet up with this fine-ass bitch I met last night. I could tell by the way she was pushing herself up on me that she wanted to fuck." I started laughing because Markese fucking a new bitch every other day was nothing new. I knew that he would die with his dick deep in some pussy.

"You need help—for real, fam."

"Yeah, ok. I bet you're about to leave here and get deep in some pussy. So, nigga, stop stunting.

I can't even lie. I'm thinking about calling up one of my freaks, not for pussy but for some long, slow head, and I know just the bitch to call. This bitch is a head doctor her head so damn fire that I don't have any other choice but to keep her on my team I said to myself.

"You a foo'—you know that?"

"Yeah, and the hos love it."

I couldn't do shit but shake my head. "All right, I'm out of here. Hit me up later, fam," I said as I jumped into my Rolls-Royce and pulled off. I lit an already-rolled blunt and dialed Tina's number. She was a little bitch I saw from time to time. All those hos wanted was a nigga with some money. I would never be a bitch come up. I knew that if I gave those hos my all, they'd leave me with nothing. I fucked them and ducked them. No woman had ever had my heart. Those bitches were quick to fuck on the first night—and I never would have made a bitch who sucked my dick before I even knew her name my wife.

"Hello," she said into the phone.

"Where you at, shorty? I'm around your way." Once she told me that she was home, I hung up the phone and headed her way.

Stonie

Once we left the house, we spent the rest of the day shopping and eating. I could get used to Chicago. I saw why Cinnamon had moved there. The food was on point, and the malls had way more than the malls in Indiana. "She might be seeing me a lot more often," I thought to myself. I love to shop. My true passion is doing hair, but if I could get paid to shop all day or get paid to shop for other people who don't have the time or know-how to put together their clothes, I would.

Once we got back to Cinnamon's place, Chyna and I decided to go out while party-pooping Cinnamon took a nap. Once she gets high and tipsy, all she can see is a bed—or the next best thing. Then she ends up saying, "I'll see you in the morning." Chyna and I were not going to waste our first night in Chicago cooped up in the house. We were dressed and ready to hit a bar, and since we didn't know our way around, we had to call a cab. We were already tipsy from the shots of Patron that we were still taking, and the Chicago traffic was horrible. A cab was the best choice for us.

"Come on, Chyna. The cabdriver called and said he's downstairs."

Everyone says I'm the slow one, but I was ready to go, and she wasn't.

"Ok, I'm ready to go. I had to put my lipstick on. Don't be rushing me because you're on time for the first time in life."

I didn't pay her comment any mind. We walked out of the house and got into the cab. I told the man that we weren't from there and that we wanted to go to a bar that played good music and would have a nice crowd. Fifteen minutes later, we were pulling up to the bar the cabdriver had chosen for us. It looked like it was packed and popping, but the line wasn't too long. We were in and seated within ten minutes.

On the way in, I couldn't help but notice this dark-skinned "dread head" sitting at the bar next to a brown-skinned dude with a fade. He kept looking at me, but I played it coo'. I could tell by his appearance that he had money. The Rolex on his wrist, the Givenchy outfit he was rocking, and the Givenchy sneakers on his feet screamed "money," but that shit didn't faze me. I had money too—maybe not as much as he had, but I wasn't broke or looking for a come up, so I didn't pay him no attention. I kept talking to Chyna, and we talked and drank for what seemed like the whole night. We didn't even notice that the bar was slowly getting empty.

I couldn't help but look to my left and see the same "dread head" still sitting at the bar. He must've caught me looking, because he got up and started walking over to our booth.

"Excuse me, ma. I hope I'm not interrupting you or anything, but do I have to keep looking at you all night to get your attention? I know you see me looking, because I keep catching you staring at me. You see something you like?"

He smiled, showing his pretty white teeth. I couldn't help but smile, knowing that this nigga had just called me out on my shit as though he hadn't been staring just as hard as I had been.

"Honestly, I was just waiting for you to get the balls to walk over here and speak." I could tell that he hadn't been expecting me to say that, because he burst out laughing.

"I can tell that y'all are not from here. My name is Markese—and yours?" he asked, holding his hand out for me to shake.

"I'm Stonie, and this is my cousin Chyna."

He shook Chyna's hand then asked if he and his cousin could join us.

Chapter Three

(Markese) No Games

It had been a long day. After I'd left the chop shop, my day had been non-stop. I had just checked on my last trap house when Dominique called and asked me to meet him at a bar. I didn't have anything better to do, and I could've used a drink. We weren't in there for thirty minutes before two females who I knew for damn sure weren't from here walked in. I had just about every bitch from every side of town, and I'd never once come across them. They both looked to be about five foot six. One had dark skin and long hair and was thick as hell. She looked like a black China doll. The other one had brown skin, short hair, a fat ass, and lips like Meagan Good's. I couldn't help but check shorty out. Her whole demeanor was saying "I'm the shit, and I know it." They were sitting at a booth not too far from where we were.

I looked over at Dominique, who looked like he was checking out the dark-skinned one. I couldn't believe that a bitch was holding his attention for that long. He usually didn't look twice at a bitch. Pussy didn't mean shit to him. He always said, "Pussy will be a nigga's biggest downfall, so you'll never see me running up behind a bitch."

"You're looking at shorty kind of hard," I said, causing him to stop looking at her. I didn't even think he knew that he was staring that much. He took a shot of Hennessy before he spoke.

"There ain't shit wrong with looking. When you see me chasing after a bitch, come holla at me."

"Shit, you might as well be chasing her, the way you were staring. I ain't never seen you look at a bitch twice, let alone stare at one the way you were just staring." He didn't respond, so I left it alone. For the next hour, we sat there and talked business. I couldn't help but notice that shorty was looking at me. I'm not one to play games. If I want something, I'm gonna go get it. I walked over to where they were sitting and introduced myself. To my surprise, she was quick on her feet and quick with her words. She didn't seem like the rest of those thirsty bitches. She seemed down to earth and like she had a little attitude. Shorty was doing something to me already, and I liked it. She introduced me to her cousin and said that it was ok for Dominique and me to sit with them. I called Dominique over to where we were and introduced him to the girls. We sat and talked until the bar closed, and I invited them to the opening of my brother's new club the next night. I exchanged numbers with Stonie, and we walked them to their cab. Once they pulled away, I gave this bitch named Brandy a call. With the kind of day I had, I needed some head and a massage.

Cinnamon

When I woke up that morning wearing the same clothes I had on the day before, I knew that Stonie had left me asleep and that they'd gone out without me. I tried to sit up, but my headache and dizziness threw my ass right back down. I rarely got hangovers, but from the time they'd gotten into town right up until I'd passed out, all we'd done was take shots of Patron. I kept feeling something vibrating in my bed. It was my phone, which was going off nonstop. Before I could even check to see who it was, I got another call.

"Hello," I said without looking to see who was calling.

"Damn, didn't you see me calling you all last night and this morning?"

I had to take the phone off of my ear and look at it to make sure that he had the right number. "Hello, Cinnamon. What, you can't hear me now?"

I pressed the "end" button and turned my phone off. I wasn't going to answer to a nigga who wasn't my man, let alone to one I wasn't fucking or sucking. The crazy thing was that I'd known that he would become a problem the first time I'd gone out with him. One night I was bored, and I let this guy named Eric take me out to eat. I sized him up quickly. Eric was one of those tender-ass niggas who felt that if he did something for you, you owed him something. When it was time to pay the bill, I made sure to pay my half of it. I didn't even want him to be able to say that he'd bought me a meal. I'd learned a long time before that everybody who comes into your life wants something from you. Whether they want something good or bad, nobody just comes into your life just to be there. There's always a reason behind it.

After that day, I stopped answering his calls—at least until this morning. Once I turned my phone off, I tried sitting up again, and that time, I didn't feel as dizzy as I had the first time. I knew that Stonie and Chyna would still be sleep—it was only nine forty-five in the morning. In the meantime, I took a shower and got dressed. On my way to the kitchen, I passed by my guest room, and they were both passed out. I could tell that they had a long night, because Chyna hadn't even bothered to wrap her hair. I don't care how tired a black woman is. She's still gonna wrap up her hair before she goes to bed—especially Chyna. Once I got into the kitchen, I started the coffee and took out three T-bone steaks with eggs, grits, and everything else that I needed to make hash browns and toast. "They'd better be glad that I have a heart and that I love them," I thought. "Otherwise, they'd be eating Froot Loops." I was halfway done cooking when I heard Stonie walk into the kitchen. She looked like she had to either throw up or shit.

"Why are you looking like that?" I asked her.

"Girl, I had a long night. We didn't get in till about five this morning. I'm surprised you didn't hear Chyna's big mouth ass throwing up nonstop."

At that point I had to stop cooking to ask just where in the hell she'd thrown up in my house.

"What do you mean, she threw up? Where the hell did she throw up?"

Chyna answered the question. "Well, if you must know, it was in the toilet. So you can fix your fucked-up face. You're in here making it seem like I was throwing up everywhere. Bitch, I only threw up twice."

"Bitch, aren't you supposed to be asleep? Why are you up?"

"Because I heard your big-ass mouth in my sleep, so I got up. Plus I smelled food cooking."

"Anyway, Cinnamon, let me fill you in on last night at the bar."

"Yeah, you hos left me, but carry on."

"Like I was saying, I met this dark-skinned dread-head nigga. He had to have been every bit of six foot one or six foot two, and he had some of the prettiest teeth I've ever seen. I swear, he was blinding a bitch with his smile."

I just shook my head because Stonie was a pure fool.

"You know, I've never had a dark-skinned nigga before. He might be the first and only, depending on how this shit goes. The only bad thing about him is that he has money. I'm not talking about a little money—his bread is long."

When I heard that, I immediately rolled my eyes. I hated niggas with money—not because they had money but because they always acted and felt like they could have any bitch they wanted or like bitches would be willing to fuck just because of the money. I thought that it was very rare to come across a nigga with money who was humble and would treat you good—unless you were with him when he was broke.

I would've taken a man who treated me like a queen over a nigga with money any day. Money will always be there. There are a million and one ways to come up with some money, but not every man has that king-like image or mentality. You have to be born a king—it has to be built into you.

"You know I hate that type of nigga."

"Yeah, you know I do too. But I wasn't sweating him at all. You know that I couldn't care less about his money. I'm going to make shit happen with or without a nigga. I ain't never been pressed for money, and I ain't never wanted a nigga with some. Long story short, he invited us to the opening of his brother's club tonight. I told him your name, and he put us on the VIP list, so we're going. I don't want any of the shit you pulled last night. I want all three of us to turn up."

I agreed to go so that she would just shut the fuck up already. Once the food was ready, we ate and talked for the next couple of hours until James called and put Chyna in a fucked-up mood. I couldn't understand why she didn't at least have friends for times like these. When Stonie told me that she'd passed up the cousin last night, I couldn't help but be a little pissed. James kept cheating on her, but I guess it's true when they say love is blind.

Chapter Four

(Dominique)
Something Different

As I cruised down the south side of Chicago in my Mercedes-Benz, I rapped along to Young Dolph's "Back against the Wall" while smoking a blunt. I had a lot on my mind and was dealing with a lot, not only in the streets but also in my personal life. Every year around this time, I felt the same way. Time is supposed to heal all pain, but I was still hurting like the shit had happened yesterday.

When I was eleven years old, I came home from school one day only to find my mother dead in her room with two bullets in her head and her eyes wide open. When I saw her body lying there, lifeless, her eyes just looking at me, I immediately called an ambulance. I knew that my mother was dead, but I had hope that they could save her. I cried and held my mother until the police arrived. They tried to ask me questions, but I had no answers for them. They tried to contact my father, but he was nowhere to be found. Weeks went by, and there still weren't any signs of my father's whereabouts, so Malik's mother, my auntie, took me in and raised me as though I were one of her own.

For months I would dream of my mother's lifeless body over and over again. Most nights I couldn't sleep because I was too scared that I would see her lying there just looking at me, dead. I eventually found out that my father had killed my mother because she'd found out that he'd been cheating and that he had a little girl she'd known nothing about. She'd wanted a divorce, and, needless to say, he hadn't. He was all, "If I can't have you, nobody can," and he killed her. Ever since I found that out, my mind has been fucked up, my soul has been pissed off, and my heart has been cold.

Over the next couple of years, I didn't do anything but read books on the human body to learn where the main arteries are located. I even learned how to stich wounds and about the different types of medicine that you should and shouldn't give a person. When I turned eighteen, I tracked down my father's whereabouts. He and the bitch he'd cheated on my mother with lived in Houston. I watched him and his family for about a month. That bitch-ass nigga had up and left my mother and me and had started a new family with his side bitch and their daughter. The little girl looked to be about seven or eight, and she looked just like me, but she was light skinned. I waited until one night when I knew that they were each in a deep sleep. I sat and watched them sleep for about twenty minutes. Then I gave them both a shot in the neck that would keep them asleep long enough for me to get them into the car and to the warehouse I planned to take them to.

Once I had them in my car, I drove about two and a half hours to an abandoned building. Once I had them inside of it and tied down, I wasted no time and got to work on his bitch. The plan had been to wait until they woke up, but I didn't think that I could listen to her screams. I grabbed some gloves, threw on an apron, and cut a deep slit into the middle of her throat, causing her whole body to jump. I watched as she bled out, not even knowing what had hit her. Once the blood flow had slowed down, I reached into her mouth and pulled her tongue through her throat. Then I cut her eyelids off and ripped her eyes from their sockets. I put glue on her lips to close her mouth. I wanted her to be smiling at him when he opened his eyes.

I sat her in front of the table that I had tied my father to so that when he woke up, she'd be looking right at him. I walked over to where I had him tied down and began to cut his eyelids off as well. I made sure to stich up his wounds so that he could see and so that the bleeding would stop. I didn't want his bitch ass to be able to blink, let alone close his eyes. I pressed a button on the table so that he would be sitting up when he decided to wake up. I was smoking a blunt and taking shots of Patron when I heard screams. I watched from a distance as he yelled and screamed at the sight of his bitch sitting in front of him with a smile on her face and her tongue hanging out of her throat but without eyelids or eyeballs. I watched him for about five more minutes before I walked over to where he was. The look on his face was priceless; all I could do was smile.

"What's the matter, Pops? Aren't you happy to see me?" I felt it was only right to ask him that. After all, he was looking at me as though he'd seen a ghost. I couldn't help myself—I started laughing when he called me "son" and begged me for help. "Son? Now I'm his son?" I thought to myself right before I walked over to him and cut out his tongue. I knelt down.

"You don't have the right to call me your son after all that you did. You killed my mother!" I whispered into his ear. Of course, he tried to pass out, but I gave him a little shot that I like to call "rush." It gives a person an adrenaline rush, preventing him from passing out. "Now, you didn't think that I was going to let you check out of here that easy, did you?" I don't know why I even bothered asking him questions—it wasn't like he could answer me with his tongue lying on the floor. I wanted him to feel the pain that I carried around with me every day because of him.

I grabbed this cutter that was kind of shaped like a V. It was the kind of cutter that you would use to cut the end of a cigar. I cut off all ten of his fingers. One by one, they hit the floor. Since his fingers had pulled the trigger, I didn't leave him with any. To stop the bleeding, I burned the wounds that had formed where his fingers had been. I wasn't ready for him to die just yet. I wanted him to see what was about to happen to him. I knew that after I was finished with his bitch, he would be begging me for forgiveness with his eyes. But I had no sympathy for him or for his bitch. I grabbed a bucketful of sulfuric acid and poured it on her. I watched the skin burn and fall off of her bones. The smell of the burning flesh alone would've caused anyone to throw up, so I wasn't surprised when I looked over at him and saw him throwing up. I walked over to him and looked him dead in the eye before I poured the acid on him.

"I'll see you in hell," I said. I never broke eye contact with him. I wanted to watch his soul leave his body, and at that very moment, a huge weight of anger was lifted off of me. Although killing them wouldn't bring back my mother, it sure helped me sleep a little better to know that she'd finally gotten justice. I waited for about an hour and then gathered up their bones and threw them in a grinder. What had been bones were then dust. I vowed that from that day on, I would never kill another woman. Truth be told, after I bagged up her body, I felt like a coward for killing a woman. But it was her fault that she was dead. If she hadn't fucked a married man, maybe she would have lived.

The only thing I felt bad about was leaving my little sister without a mother or a father. I would never hurt a child. She had nothing to do with it. I've kept tabs on her throughout the years, and I even send her money anonymously so that she can live good instead of struggling her way through life.

I snapped out of my thoughts as I pulled up to the bar. I still had business to handle with Markese, so I hit him up and told him to meet me there. To my surprise, he was there within thirty minutes. We sat, talked, and drank—until two females walked through the door. The dark-skinned one caught my eye. There was something about her that made me do a double take. I wasn't one to sweat a bitch or to step to one, for that matter.

Pussy didn't mean shit to me. I had my fair share of women from different races. I thought that bitches were just looking for the next rich dick to either suck or ride. I'd never put my trust in a bitch. The only women I'd ever loved were my mother and my auntie. No bitch knew where I laid my head or even knew my whole name, for that matter. Shit, come to think of it, I'd never even woken up next to a bitch before. I'd fuck one and then leave. I didn't have shit for a bitch but some hard dick, if that.

I must've been looking at shorty for a minute, because Markese called me out on it. I just blew him off, but of course, that nigga walked over to their booth and started rapping with shorty's friend. Not even five minutes later, he called me over to their booth. I'm not going to stunt—I wanted to meet shorty. When I got over to their booth, I introduced myself while Markese rapped with shorty's cousin. I could tell that shorty had something on her mind. Body language is a muthafucka, and I studied people for a living. The body will talk before the mouth has even opened.

"What's on your mind, shorty? You want to talk about it?" I asked. But she just looked at me with her face screwed up.

"When you shook my hand, what did I tell you my name was?" Before I could answer, she started talking again. "I told you it was Chyna, right? Not shorty or something else. And to answer your question, my man is on my mind."

I just smirked. "Well, Ms. Chyna, I don't give a fuck about your man. You ought to tell that nigga to stop mind fucking you. Then you wouldn't look so stressed out."

She just looked at me for a minute.

"You're right. He may mind fuck me from time to time, but he's better at actually fucking me."

We locked eyes for what seemed like forever. I was getting ready to respond when the waiter came over to say that it was closing time. We all got up and headed for the door. Once we were outside, I flagged down a cab for them. I couldn't help but check out shorty as she stood there, waiting on the cabdriver to come to a complete stop. She had a perfect shape, and I could tell that her ass was real by the way she walked.

"I'll see you around," I said right before she got in the cab.

"Likewise" was all she said. Then she got in the cab, and it pulled away.

Chyna

When I woke up to the smell of someone cooking and to the sound of Stonie's loud mouth talking, I knew that it would only be a matter of time before one of the two came walking in to wake me up. With the kind of night I'd had and the hangover I was dealing with, all I wanted to do was sleep. Once I had brushed my teeth and washed my face, I headed into the kitchen, and all I could hear was Stonie's big mouth telling Cinnamon that I'd been throwing up the night before, I swear, that bitch could over-exaggerate any story. I had to correct her—I'd only thrown up twice. My head was still hurting, and I didn't have time for a back-and-forth with Stonie.

After we ate we sat and talked for a few hours. I didn't know why, but I'd woken up with Dominique on my mind. There was something about him that I just couldn't seem to figure out. I felt like he was the one who had mind fucked me, and he'd left me curious. He must have been at least six foot one, he had a fade, and his facial hair was lined up to a tee. Just by looking at his body frame, I could tell that his body was cut and that he worked out. I was so deep in my thoughts of him that I never heard my phone go off.

"Chyna, you don't hear your phone going off?" Cinnamon asked me.

I snapped out of my thoughts and walked over toward the kitchen to answer my phone. I tried to see who'd been blowing me up, but before I could call anyone back, my phone began to ring again—and that time, the call was from a blocked number.

"Hello," I said.

"Bitch, you've got me all fucked up. I know you've seen my calls all night and morning, and now you answer when a muthafucka starts calling from a private number? And you wonder why I treat you the way I do, bitch."

I couldn't have gotten a word out if I'd wanted to. I let him finish what he had to say, because I didn't have much to say.

"You're quiet now, huh? Ain't got shit to say now, do you?"

"Yeah, I got a couple of things to say. Have your broke, disrespectful ass out of my shit by the time I touch back down at home, or I'm gonna have a muthafucka come drag you out."

I hung the phone up and turned it off. "I've dealt with his broke, insecure ass for long enough," I thought to myself as I walked to the back and shut the door. Truth be told, I wanted to cry. No matter what a woman and her nigga have been through, no woman truly wants to end shit with him. But not everybody has had to deal with the type of nigga that I was dealing with. I'd known that this day would come, but I'd hoped like hell that it wouldn't hurt the way it did. After I'd shed the last tears that I would ever shed over him, I walked back to the living room and thanked God that Stonie was rolling a blunt. I needed it. I felt like Pac—like all eyes were on me. The last thing I wanted to do was sit and talk about what had just gone down with James.

"Y'all are just lying around. Let's get out the house. I need to find me a dress for tonight."

"Didn't you just bring half of the mall back with you yesterday? I know you've got something in those bags that you can throw on," Cinnamon said while flipping through the options on Netflix.

"Yeah, but I'm trying to walk up out of there tonight with something new on my team."

"Bitch, please. The only nigga you're checking for is that broke-ass nigga you left back in Nap."

I was already pissed off, and Stonie wasn't making it any better. I had no control over what came out my mouth next.

"Bitch, I'm not in the mood for your wack-ass comments. Everybody and their mama know about James. Every time some shit happens between us, you have to butt in with your two cents. Next time, keep it to yourself, because I don't give a damn about what the fuck you have to say about my relationship. Like your shit was any better."

"Well, excuse the fuck out of me. Here—take the blunt. It's clear that you need it more than I do. I don't give a fuck about your relationship—or whatever the fuck you want to call it. I wouldn't know anything about y'all if you hadn't come to me crying about your relationship. I never said my relationship was any better, but at least I had sense enough to leave and to not get dogged by him. So excuse me if I don't want to see my cousin go through bullshit that she doesn't have to go through. I know you're better than that so, yeah, fuck you too, bitch. And it's 'puff, puff, pass,' not 'sit and hold the blunt,' bitch."

"Fuck you, Stonie."

"Yeah, I love you too, bitch. Now pass the blunt."

I passed the blunt over to Cinnamon, who, to my surprise, had nothing to say about the situation. She just grabbed the blunt.

"Are you bitches done yet? I could be getting my pussy waxed, but here I am, listening to you two bitches arguing over nothing."

Stonie and I must have been thinking the same thing, because on cue, we both said, "Shut the fuck up."

"Whatever. You bitches can get to stepping. Take a look around. This is all my shit. Don't let the door hit you hos on the way out."

We all started to laugh because Cinnamon didn't "have it all." I honestly didn't have a clue where she came from. After talking for about an hour, we showered and headed out.

Chapter Five

(Malik)
Angel Out of Heaven

It was the night of the big opening of my club. I already owned two res-
taurants and a strip club. I had to turn my dirty money into clean money
somehow, so I invested in my own businesses. Most of my money was
legit. I was on my way to "Brenda's" when Markese hit me up. "Brenda"
was the name of my main trap house, where more than half of my money
was made. I also had two other trap houses called "Pam" and "Peaches,"
but I loved Brenda like a fat kid loves cake.

"What's up?" I said, answering the phone.

"Nothing much. Making a few last-minute plays. Where you at, fam?"

"I'm headed to see Brenda. I have to count this paper before I do
anything else."

"Ok. I swung by Peaches' crib earlier. Shit's slapping that way."

"Yeah. I love to hear that."

"I know. Are you ready for tonight, fam? You know that I'm leave with
at least two bitches tonight. Speaking of bitches, fam, last night I went to

the bar to meet up with Dominique. I wasn't in there for longer than thirty or forty minutes at the most, and then two bad bitches from out of town walked in. You know I've had my fair share, so believe me when I tell you that those hos were bad. I can tell that the shorty I wanted is gonna be a little hard to get. I'm gonna have to wine and dine the panties off of her. I put them on the VIP list, so hopefully, they'll come through tonight."

All I could do was laugh at my brother.

"Nigga, I swear that you need to look into sex rehab."

"Yeah, you may be right. But as long as I can get hard and stay cocked, nigga, I'm gonna be dropping dick on my deathbed." We both started laughing and then continued to talk until I pulled up to Brenda's.

"All right, fam. I'll catch you later at the club."

I hung the phone up as I drove up to "see Brenda." When I pulled up, I spotted Choppa's and Zilla's cars parked out front. Choppa is my little nigga who I used to sling heavy with on the corner when we were little niggas. He ended up catching a case and doing four years. As soon as he touched down, I "put" him on. He got the name "Choppa" because that little nigga stayed with one and wasn't afraid to let that chopper squirt. Zilla is his little brother. Now, that little nigga is wild. He doesn't give any fucks. He shoots, and he doesn't ask questions later. Both of those niggas are like family to me. They've been nothing but loyal since I met them. That's why I don't mind breaking bread with them.

As I walked through the trap, I saw ass-naked bitches breaking down bricks, cooking, and bagging that shit up. My trap wasn't one of those dirty-ass traps that you have to kick your way through. It was clean and completely furnished. I didn't want it to seem like a trap house if the pigs ever came. I had places all over to hide my shit. I had walls that came out and a safe that was underground. Those muthafuckas would have a hell of a time trying to kick in a front door made of metal, and I would need that extra time to stash or flush what I had. I walked to the basement, where Choppa and Zilla were. They were counting money and smoking a blunt.

"What's up, fam?" I dapped both of them.

"Same shit, different day. Just chasing paper," Zilla said while passing me the blunt.

"You ready for tonight, fam? With the way my week's been going, there ain't no telling what I'll get into," Choppa said.

"Yeah, shit's going to be live."

"Good, because I could use a little freaky ho to ease my mind." I didn't know who was worse—Markese or this nigga. The only difference was that Choppa had a bitch at home.

"Nigga, didn't Brittany just catch you at the strip club last week, and didn't she fuck you and the bitch you had with you up? Nigga, why you want to go and do that again?"

"I'm not worried about Brittany. As long as I'm taking care of her, I don't see what the problem is. She knew what kind of nigga I was before she even got involved with me. I buy her everything she wants, I put her in a nice-ass crib, and I try my best to leave the little shit I do in the dark. But she goes looking for shit, so that's on her."

I had nothing to say to that. I just hoped she wouldn't pop up tonight. I didn't care who she was—I'd throw her ass out. After we counted all of the money, we threw it into five big duffel bags. I took three with me. One was for me, and the other two were for Dominique and Markese. Once I was in my car, I headed to my crib. When I pulled up to it, I punched in the code and waited till the gates opened. I'm a king, so it's only right that I have a house made for a king. After I showered and got dressed, it was a little after midnight. I rolled a blunt and headed out.

On the way to the club, I smoked my blunt and listened to Boosie's "Streetz Iz Mine." When I pulled up to the street my club was on, a line was wrapped around the building. "Say my name, and the whole city comes out," I thought to myself. When I walked into the club, all I could see were strippers hanging from the ceiling and dancing. I had three VIP sections and a upstairs section for the niggas who wanted a private booth with the strippers. Once I made my way past the crowd of people, I headed upstairs to my own VIP section, where I could see everything happening in my club. When I walked through the doors, Choppa, Zilla, Markese, and Dominique were already up there with a roomful of naked strippers dancing. They were making it rain on them hos. I walked around and gave them all some dap.

"Aye, fam, this shit is wild. Where'd you find these bitches?" Choppa asked

"I flew them in from all over." I hadn't wanted just any strippers, so I'd flown in about fifty exotic strippers of all different races from all over the country. I had some of the baddest strippers shaking their asses.

"I plan on taking that freaky-ass Jamaican home with me, fam."

"Do your thang, fam." Shit, with the way she was shaking her ass, I could see why he wanted her. I'd made sure to have an open bar with nonstop bottle service the whole night for my team and me. After the way we'd been working, we deserved it. I was smoking a blunt and getting a lap dance when Markese walked in with three females I'd never seen before. They were all bad, but the one in all white stood out to me the most. Shorty had a glow to her that was very rare, and the all-white outfit she was wearing made her look godly. Markese hadn't been lying when he'd said that he'd met some bad bitches. I looked over at Dominique, who, to my surprise, kept looking at the dark-skinned one. He was the last nigga who I thought would be eyeballing any bitch. Based on the way he was looking at shorty, I could tell that he wanted her. I watched as Markese walked over to where I was.

"Aye, fam, these are the ladies I told you I met last night. This is Stonie, and these are her cousins, Chyna and Cinnamon. Ladies, this is my big brother, Malik, and this is his club."

I stood up so that I could shake hands with the girls. "It's nice to meet you beautiful ladies. I hope y'all will enjoy yourselves. There's an open bar—please help yourself. If you need anything, just let me or the other guys know, and we'll get it for you." I watched as shorty and the dark-skinned one headed to a booth while the other shorty sat down and talked to Markese. I didn't know what it was about shorty, but I couldn't stop looking at her. The other two seem coo', but she seemed so nonchalant. It was like she didn't even want to hold a conversation with a nigga. Maybe she had a nigga, but I didn't give a fuck about whether she had a man. I was trying to get to know her. I had every intention of stepping to her, but it would be on my time.

Cinnamon

We spent most of the day at the spa getting pampered. I figured that with the kind of morning we'd had, we all needed a massage. By the time we headed back to my house, it was going on ten thirty, and we began to shower and get dressed for the night. I planned on having fun tonight, since I'd been left behind the night before. As we got dressed, we passed a few blunts around and took a few shots of Patron. Once we were dressed, we looked like a million bucks. Actually, fuck it—make that a billion bucks. I decided on an all-white minidress with some red open-toe heels to go along with it. Chyna wore an all-black lace dress that hugged her thick-ass shape and showed off all of her curves, and Stonie went with a two-piece cream dress that made her ass look superfat. I mean, it was already big, but the way it sat up in that dress would've put any bitch with ass shots to shame.

"I must say that I have some badass cousins," I said to myself as we headed out the door and jumped in Stonie's all-black Range Rover. On the way to the club, we bumped Kevin Gates's "Really Really." We weren't even at the club yet, and we were already turned up and rapping along with Gates. Once we pulled up to the club, there was a line wrapped around the building and no place to even park. Stonie must have texted the guy who'd invited us, because not even five minutes later, a man walked up to our car and gave us a VIP pass so that we could park on the other side of the building. Once we'd parked, we headed inside, where a tall, nice-looking dark-skinned dread head was waiting for us.

"For a minute, I thought you weren't going to come," he said while hugging Stonie.

"I'm sorry. It took us a while to get dressed. You met my cousin Chyna last night. This is my other cousin Cinnamon—I was telling you about her."

"You're straight, ma. Nice to meet you, Cinnamon. I'm Markese," he said while reaching out to shake my hand.

"Nice to meet you, Markese. Thank you for the invite." Stonie hadn't been lying when she'd said that you could tell that his money was long. He looked like a walking bankroll. All I could do was shake my head. I'll never understand why niggas feel the need to be so flashy.

"Thank y'all for coming. Follow me. We're going to take the sideway to my private room so that you won't have to walk through the crowd of people." As we followed him down a hall and up some stairs, I could see the crowd of people and all of the strippers who were hanging from the ceiling and dancing. The whole scene was like some never-before-seen shit. Once we got to the second floor, all we could see were more naked strippers giving private dances.

We continued to walk until we came to two double doors. You had to punch in a code to get through them. Once the doors had opened, we saw that there was a whole other party going on with different music being played, flat-screen TVs everywhere, a bar just as big as the one downstairs, and even more strippers dancing. I looked over to where the strippers were dancing. Most of the floor was covered with money. We continued to walk until we came to a man who was getting a lap dance. He had some of the smoothest chocolate skin I'd ever seen, a fade full of waves, and a lineup that would've put Steve Harvey's to shame.

Once he stood up, I took in his whole appearance. He had to be every bit of six foot two, and he had a muscular shape. He kind of reminded me of Morris Chestnut when he played in the movie *Best Man*. Everything he had on was Versace, and he had a big-faced Rolex on his wrist. After Markese introduced us, Chyna and I went to a booth and sat down while Stonie talked with Markese. There were more niggas in the room, but I couldn't have cared less. I hadn't come to mingle—I'd come to party and to have fun. Besides, every nigga in the room screamed "money," and that nigga Malik screamed it the loudest. I caught him looking at me a few times, but I just hit my blunt and laughed to myself. Niggas with money always want what they can't have. I didn't pay his ass no attention. I would be lying if I said I didn't think he was fine as hell, but I knew his type, and I didn't want any part of it.

Gucci Mane's "Nothing On Ya" came on, and I couldn't help myself—I got up and started dancing. I was tipsy as hell—not to mention the fact that that's one of my favorite songs. I rapped along with Gucci while I danced: "They ain't got nothing on ya. I swear them hos ain't got nothing on ya. I fuck with you 'cause you're very loyal, and you're so fine you make my blood boil." I made sure to look them strippers up and down while I rapped along, and I still felt like those bitches didn't have shit on my cousins and me. Chyna got up and started dancing with me. Chyna could dance her ass off if not better than the strippers. We were definitely feeling ourselves. After the song finished, we sat back down. I could tell that Chyna had a thing for the tall brown-skinned nigga with the fade—I don't miss shit. They both kept looking at each other.

"You know, if you're going to keep looking at him, you should go over there and talk to him." She gave me a look that said, "Bitch, I wouldn't dare."

"He sees me just like I see him. If he wants me bad enough, he'll step to me."

"Bitch, are we in high school? What're y'all going to do—keep looking at each other and hoping that somebody gets the balls to speak first?"

She just shrugged her shoulders and said, "I guess so." I swear, Chyna is one stubborn-ass person. A nigga other than James had her attention, and she wanted to play games. I guess the saying "to each his own" is true. I watched as Stonie walked over to where we were, looking like she wasn't happy.

"Is this what you hos came to do—sit down the whole night and look around? Y'all should be mingling and having fun. You bitches should have stayed at home if this is how y'all are going to be acting."

"Stonie, you know I'm not a people person, so miss me with that bullshit you're talking," I said.

"Ain't nobody telling y'all to go fuck those niggas, but at least mingle and chitchat with them—that's all I'm asking." I looked over at Chyna, whose face looked like she didn't care about what Stonie was talking about.

"Come on, Chyna. Let's go over there so that this cry baby–ass bitch will shut up."

"Fuck you, Cinnamon, but thank you. Now come on." We both got up and followed Stonie back to where everyone was. I sat down next to Chyna, who didn't sit there for long. She finally stopped playing games and went to talk to Markese's cousin. I bobbed my head to the music that was playing. I was bored, sitting up there with those niggas. Hell, the real party was going on downstairs. Just when I was getting ready to get up and tell Chyna that I was going downstairs, Malik walked over to me, and for some strange reason, I had butterflies in my stomach. I couldn't remember the last time a man had made me feel like that.

"What's wrong, ma? Just a minute ago, you were up dancing and having fun, what happened that fast?" For a moment I just looked at him. He was very handsome and smelled good as hell.

"Yeah, that's because the real party is going on downstairs. I was just about to get up and head down there when you walked over here." He just smiled a little and stared me down. I felt like he was eye fucking me, the way he was looking at me and licking his lips.

"Why are you looking at me like that?" I asked him.

"Do I make you feel uncomfortable?" he asked, never breaking eye contact with me.

"No, but if you're going to just sit there and stare at me, you can watch me while I'm on the dance floor," I said as I walked away to tell Chyna that I was going downstairs. On the way to the door, I looked over at Malik, who was still standing where I'd left him. He was just looking at me with a smirk on his face. I didn't know what it was about that man, but he was doing something to me that no man had been able to do in the past few months, and that's get my attention.

Malik

Watching shorty dancing from a distance only made me wanna step to her more. The way her ass moved in that dress and her whole demeanor caught my attention. I'd known that I wanted her from the time she'd walked in with Markese, but when I went to talk to shorty, she cut the conversation short. Just after the little conversation we'd had, I could tell that she had a smart mouth and an "I don't give a fuck" attitude, but it was nothing I couldn't handle. But I'm not the type of nigga who's going to chase after a bitch, so when shorty walked away, I let her know that I wasn't pressed for pussy, especially not in a room full of ass-naked bitches who were willing to go.

I was taking shots of Hennessy and throwing money on this Spanish stripper who was giving me a lap dance when Tina came walking in. I'd forgotten that I'd put her on the VIP list so that she would shut the fuck up and stop asking me about it. Tina wasn't my bitch or even the closest thing to it—she was just a bitch I saw from time to time. I watched her as she looked around the room, trying to find me. Once she spotted me, she walked over to where I was and politely asked the stripper to move. Shorty had life fucked up if she thought that I wasn't going to finish get-ting my dance. The stripper looked at me like she was going to stop.

"What're you doing, shorty? Don't you see me getting a dance right now? You can either wait till she's done, or you can come bounce that ass on this dick. Either way, I'm gonna finish getting this dance." I could tell that she was pissed off, but I didn't care. I gave her a choice: if she wanted the stripper to stop, then she had to take her place. She just walked over to a booth with her arms crossed. Once I was done getting my dance, I waved for her to come back over. She looked like she had an attitude when she walked over. "I don't have time for this shit tonight," I thought to myself.

"Aye, ma, why's your face all twisted up and shit? You can lose your fucked-up attitude, or you can leave."

"I don't have an attitude, zaddy," she said, sitting on my lap.

I looked over at Choppa, who was walking out with one of the strippers. I just shook my head. "His bitch is going to body bag both of them if she finds out," I thought to myself. I snapped out of my thoughts when I felt Tina rubbing on my dick through my pants.

"Zaddy, she's calling for you," she whispered in my ear as she took my hand and moved it up her dress, making me feel how wet her pussy was. Tina was a freak at heart—shorty was always on some freaky shit. No matter where she was, she was ready to fuck or to suck some dick. I planned on fucking the shit out of her the moment we left the club. When I pulled my hand out from underneath her dress, she grabbed my hand and sucked her juices off of my fingers. I never saw Cinnamon walk back into the room—she had been gone for most of the night, and I hadn't been expecting her to come back. She just looked at me and kept walking over to where the other girls were. It didn't bother me that she was in the room, but I would be lying if I said that I didn't look over at her a few times. She looked like she didn't have a care in the world as she bobbed her head to the music. Once the club had closed and I had counted all of the money I'd made that night, I followed Tina back to her house. Before I could even get in the house all of the way, she pulled my dick out and went to work.

Chapter Six

(Cinnamon)
A Month Later

I was checking on my last patient when Chyna texted me to say that she was at my house. She'd been in town every weekend since she'd met Dominique. I could honestly say that I liked him for her—he seemed cool and good for her. I couldn't remember the last time I'd seen Chyna that happy. I gathered my things and clocked out, and on my way out the door, I bumped into Markese. He did a double take before he spoke.

"What's up, Cinnamon? I thought that was you. What are you doing up here?" he asked.

"What's up, Markese? And as you can see, I work here. I should be asking you what you're doing here." He laughed a little while shaking his head.

"Do all of y'all have that smart-ass mouth? And to answer your question, my boy Zilla just had a baby, and I'm here to show my support."

"Well, that's nice of you. Tell the couple that I said congratulations on the baby."

"Ok, I will. And tell your cousin Stonie to hit a nigga back. Shorty just gave me the cold shoulder for nothing." I looked at him like he was stupid. I wasn't a damn messenger.

"Nigga, what do I look like—cupid? You can tell her yourself."

He looked at me and started to laugh. "Damn, ma. You cold for that."

"Yeah, whatever. I'll think about telling her."

"All right, good looking. Take care, ma."

"Yeah, you too."

Once I was outside, I got into my car and pulled away. I worked fifteen minutes away from my house, so it didn't take me long to get home. When I walked in, Chyna was sitting on the couch, smoking a blunt, and watching *Love & Hip Hop: Atlanta*.

"What's up?" she asked as she passed me the blunt.

"Same shit, different day. What do you have planned for tonight? Let's go get some drinks or something."

"I can't tonight—I have plans with Dominique."

I just rolled my eyes. "Great," I thought to myself.

"But Choppa is having a birthday bash tomorrow night. You don't have to work, so there's no reason for you not to come. As a matter of fact, bitch, you are going."

"Last time I checked, my mama lived in Indianapolis," I thought to myself.

"Well, ok, Mama Chyna. If you say so." Truth be told, I wanted to go. I hadn't been able to stop thinking about Malik since the day I'd met him. I had no real reason to think of him the way I did, especially since we hadn't had a real conversation. And yet he was still on my mind. Considering all of the hos he had, though, I was sure that I hadn't crossed his mind once. I got up and began to head for the back of the house.

"Where you going?" Chyna asked.

"To wash my ass. Do you want to watch, since you're playing mama today?"

She laughed and stuck her middle finger up. "You're the true definition of an asshole."

"Yeah, well, tell me something I don't know."

Once I was out of the shower, dry, and dressed, I walked to the kitchen to take out something to cook for the night. I had no plans and no real friends other than my cousins. I didn't fuck with bitches. I'd found out the hard way that hanging out with the wrong kinds of bitches only causes drama, and I didn't need that in my life. There was one girl I worked with who I talked to here and there, but I didn't consider her a friend—she was just cool to talk to. I walked over to the living room, where Chyna was, and sat down.

"I forgot to tell you who I bumped into today when I was leaving work—it was that nigga Markese. He asked me to tell Stonie to hit him up, because she gave him the cold shoulder—or some shit like that."

"Well, I doubt that'll happen. She said that when they went out on a date, he just kept looking at other bitches. I'm not talking about just glancing at them—she said he was staring at them like she wasn't even sitting right there."

I shook my head. "That's some disrespectful-ass shit. I told y'all that them type of nigga has no respect for women."

"Well, I don't have that problem with Dominique. He's a lot different than they are. And besides, we're still at the stage of getting to know each other, so if some shit like that does happen, it won't be a big deal for me to drop him."

"I know that's right." For the next couple of hours, we sat and talked—that is, until Chyna left with Dominique, leaving me all by my lonesome. After I cooked and ate, I rolled a blunt, poured a glass of wine, and listened to SoMo's "Ride." I found myself thinking about Malik. What was it about that man that made me think about him night and day? I'd told myself that I'd never fall for his type, and there I was with him on my mind yet again.

Malik

"Everywhere I go, I got good crack. Swagger to dope bitch, she eat it up. Cook up the crack, watch them eat it up. Trap in the spot till the lease up." I was rapping along with Peewee Longway's "Good Crack" as I drove to the hospital to meet baby Zilla. I was happy for my little nigga. Kids are a blessing. I will never understand how a nigga couldn't be in his child's life. I was proud of my little nigga. He'd been going hard ever since he'd found out that he had a little Zilla on the way—not to mention the fact that he had a down-ass bitch who he'd been with for years. There ain't nothing like having a family with the one you truly love.

Once I got to the hospital, I took the elevator up to the labor-and-delivery floor. When I got to their room, I knocked on the door and waited till I heard her say "come in." When I walked in, I saw that Markese, Choppa, and Shantel's sister, Amber, were there. She was the last bitch I wanted to see. I'd fucked shorty a little while back, and she'd gotten on some crazy-clingy shit. I'd had to cut shit off with shorty. I'd told her how it would be from the jump. If she couldn't handle it, she shouldn't have let me fuck her.

"Congratulations" I said, hugging Zilla and then giving him some dap.

"Right on, fam. Thanks for coming."

"You know I wouldn't miss this shit for nothing, fam." I walked over to Shantel's bed and handed her some balloons that I'd stopped to get on my way up and a bagful of clothes for baby Zilla.

"Congratulations," I said while handing her the gifts.

"Thank you, Malik. I really appreciate everything."

"You're welcome. You know y'all are my family. Anything for my nephew."

Since Choppa had the baby, I walked over to him, not paying Amber any attention. The bitch just kept eyeballing me. I didn't have shit to say to her. It would be a cold day in hell before I'd ever fuck her crazy ass again. I gave Markese some dap.

"What's up, fam?"

"You already know, fam. Same shit."

I looked over at Choppa, who was sitting next to Markese, who was then holding the baby. "What's up, fam? Let me see my nephew. You're over here taking over and shit."

He started laughing. "Hell, yeah, fam. This little nigga stole my heart already." I could understand why Choppa and Zilla didn't have families. They'd both been raised by their grandmother, who'd passed away a few years before. So all they really had was each other. He handed me the baby, and all I could do was smile. The little nigga looked just like Zilla. It's crazy how you can plant your seed in a woman, and then the baby comes out looking just like you. That shit is amazing to me. After visiting with them awhile, Markese and I headed out. I still had business to handle regarding my restaurant and my strip club. Once we were outside in the parking lot, I was getting ready to hop into my car when he started talking.

"Oh yeah, I forgot to tell you that I ran into shorty from your party earlier today—you know, that Cinnamon chick. Aye, fam, shorty has a smart-ass mouth on her, fam. Somebody either needs to shut her up or put something in it, if you know what I mean."

I will never understand my brother—that nigga's just wild.

"Yeah, well, let another nigga deal with that. I'm not gonna chase no bitch. I don't give a damn how bad she is."

"I feel you on that, fam, because shorty's badder than a muthafucka."

"You ain't never lied. All right, fam. I'm out of here. I've got shit to do. Hit me up later." After giving him some dap, I jumped in my Benz and pulled away. I'm not gonna stunt—Cinnamon had crossed my mind from time to time, but shorty had another think coming if she thought that I was going to chase her. The only things I would chase were commas. As

I pulled up to my restaurant, I could see that we had a full house. When I walked in, I went straight to my office to check inventory and to order anything we needed. I was putting in an order when I heard a knock on my door.

"Come in." I knew it could only be one person, and that was Kim.

I'd hired her to run the restaurant when I was out. Kim was a bad red bone with long hair and a fat ass. Like Boosie said, "Mama white, daddy black, so that ass is super fat." I would never fuck Kim, though. I don't mix business with pleasure. I'd hired her because of her business degree and her ability to run my restaurant as if it were her own. I'd be lying if I said that I'd never thought about hitting that. Hell, one time she tried to throw me the pussy. It took everything I had to not bend her over across my desk and knock that pussy out of the frame. I had to let little mama know that our relationship would be strictly business but that if eventually, she stopped working for me, I'd be more than willing to bless her one time.

"I'm sorry, I didn't mean to bother you. I was just checking to see if you needed anything." I gave her the once-over. She looked good in the all-black outfit she was rocking, and the skirt she had on hugged her shape and made her ass sit up just right. The red-bottom shoes she had on gave her a little height. I love a woman who takes pride in her appearance.

"Thank you, Kim, but I'm fine. I'm going to finish ordering everything we need and then head over to the club. I appreciate that, though."

"You're welcome. I'll be up front in case you need me." I watched as she walked out the door, swinging her ass. Temptation is a muthafucka. After taking care of payroll and everything else, I headed out to the club.

Dominique

As I cruised the highway with Chyna, I smoked a blunt and listened to her rap along with Future's "Real Sisters." We had just left the best Italian restaurant in the Chi, and to my surprise, she didn't want to go home. I knew that Chyna was different, so taking her to my crib didn't matter to me. I knew everything there was to know about her from the things she'd told me and from some shit that I'd found out on my own. With the kind of life, I was living, I had to know just who I was dealing with. When we pulled up to my crib, I put in the code and waited till the gates opened. Once we were far enough in to see my house, I could tell that she hadn't expected to see such a big-ass house.

"Damn, your house is huge. Why do you have this big-ass house just for you?"

"After growing up where I did and with the type of life that I was forced to live, as soon as I got my first big lump of money, I bought this house and paid in cash. It's fit for a real king."

Once we were inside, I gave her a full tour of my house. I had eight bedrooms, a movie theater, two living rooms, a basement, a man cave, and a game room. After showing her around, I grabbed a bottle of Hennessy and some Patron. She followed me back to my room and sat on the bed. I poured each of us a shot. I watched as she got up and headed to the bathroom. Moments later, she was calling my name.

"Dominique, how the hell do you turn your shower on? And do you have anything that I could put on?" I cut the shower on for her and brought back one of my T-Shirts and a pair of boxers. When I walked in, she was already in the shower. To make matters worse, the shower was made of glass, so I could see everything. She turned around and stuck her head out of the shower.

"Thank you. Just set it on the counter, please." She stuck her head back in and continued to wash up. She acted as if it didn't faze her that I could see that she was naked. I set the clothes down and walked out. Twenty minutes later she walked out of the bathroom fully dressed. Chyna had my dick rock hard, and all I could do was get up and walk it off.

"Where you going?" she asked while getting into the bed.

"I'm about to hop in the shower. Make yourself comfortable. There's a jar of weed in the top dresser. Take some if you want to smoke." I walked to the bathroom to take my shower. When I came out, Chyna was in bed watching *Juice*. I couldn't do shit but laugh. She was always watching some gangster-ass movie. She must have heard me, because she looked up.

"What you know about this movie, ma?"

"The same things you know—maybe more," she replied. Chyna had a smart-ass mouth, and I planned on handling that when the time was right. I can't front, though—I kind of liked it. Once I was in the bed, she just laid her head on my chest and fired up the blunt that she must have rolled when I was in the shower. For the rest of the night, we talked about everything. I sat and listened to her vent about her life and about the things she'd been through.

I could tell that Chyna had a good heart. Just listening to her talk, you could hear the pain in her voice. I didn't understand why shorty had let that nigga shit on her the way he had. I could have easily taken advantage of her—she seemed so vulnerable—but I liked Chyna. She was the only woman I'd ever brought to my house or opened up to—period. I wanted her to see the differences between other niggas and me. If we ever took it to the next level, it would be because she wanted to.

I went on to tell her about my mother and about me finding her dead at a young age. We talked about what I did for a living in the streets. To my surprise, she didn't judge me. Her main concern was my safety and freedom. Shorty really didn't know the kind of nigga she dealing with. Safety was the last thing I was worried about, and the police would've had to get close enough to me to catch me if they wanted to just take me in. I was always ten steps ahead of them in everything I did, so that was the last thing I was worried about. It was going on four in the morning when Chyna started to doze off. I wasn't sure if she wanted to lie with me or in the guest room, so I tapped her to wake her up.

"Aye, ma, are you going to sleep with me or in the guest room?"

She gave me a look that said "Nigga, you woke me up for this?"

"Where have I been all night?" she said before laying her head back on my chest and falling asleep.

"Chyna is a piece of work," I thought to myself. I was glad that shorty was staying in bed with me. It felt good to lie next to her. For the next hour, I watched her sleep with her head on my chest and her arm across my stomach. For the first time all night, shorty looked peaceful and stress-free. Moments later I was falling asleep myself.

Chapter Seven

(Chyna) Checked

Waking up next to Dominique had me feeling some type of way. I'd slept good for the first time in a long time, and to my surprise, he never made a move on me. The whole night we'd sat and talked while smoking a few blunts. I couldn't remember the last time I had a real conversation with a nigga who'd wanted to hear about my life and me and hadn't just wanted to fuck. He listened to me vent all night and even opened up to me about his father murdering his mother. I felt bad for him because he had no family other than Malik and Markese. He'd been through so much at a young age that it affected him as an adult. I understood why he acted the way he did. I rolled over and got out of bed and headed to the bathroom to at least wash my face. If I'd known that I was going to stay over, I would have packed an overnight bag. When I came out of the bathroom, he was sitting on the edge of the bed and was talking on the phone. Once he was done with his phone call, he looked over at me with a smile.

"Good morning, ma. How did you sleep last night?"

"Good morning, and I slept good—it was the best sleep I've had in a long time."

"That's good. I'm glad to hear that. Well, I called my auntie's assistant and gave her all of your sizes. She'll come over with some clothes for you to wear, since you don't have any here to put on for the day. In the meantime, I do have an extra brand-new toothbrush that you can use."

"Thank you for the toothbrush, but you didn't have to buy me any clothes. I could have gone and grabbed some from Cinnamon's house."

He stood up and walked over to where I was and looked me dead in the eye.

"It will be a cold day in hell before I'll let you walk out of my house with nothing but a T-Shirt and some boxers on, ma. And I don't need your permission to do shit. You didn't have any clothes, so I made sure that you did. You'll find out sooner or later that I'm nothing like your last nigga. The sooner you realize that, the better off we're going to be. Now, can a nigga get something to eat in the meantime? Shit, I'm hungry."

I'm not going to lie—for the first time in my life, I didn't have shit to say. I felt like I couldn't have said shit even if I'd had something to say. He'd just checked the hell out of me, and all I could do was go brush my teeth and then feed him like he'd asked me to. I couldn't help but steal a peek of him shirtless in the mirror with all of those damn tattoos on his chest and back. I hadn't gotten a good look at them the night before. I never would've known that he was tatted up the way he was. He smirked at me in the mirror as he washed his face.

"You see something you like, ma? You're staring kind of hard and shit." I didn't know I was staring the way I was until he said something. That nigga was just too cocky for his own good.

"Yeah, I see a whole lot that I like." I smiled and winked at him and headed downstairs to the kitchen to cook for him. When I got to the kitchen, I didn't know where to start. The kitchen was so damn big that it took me ten minutes to find all of the pots and pans that I needed. For a man with no woman, he sure had a kitchen full of food and cooking tools. I began to cut up some fruit to make a fruit tray. I didn't know what he liked to eat, so I decided to make everything: ham, sausage, steak, bacon, eggs, girts, pancakes, hash browns, fried potatoes, and fresh orange juice. Hell, he could decide what he wanted to eat when it was done. As I cooked, I listened to Aaliyah's Pandora station. I sang alone to the songs as I cooked—that is, until I heard the doorbell ring. I wasn't sure who it was, and I wasn't about to answer the door. Moments later, Dominique came walking into the kitchen with some light-skinned mixed bitch with bags in her hand.

"Chyna, this is Ashley, my auntie's assistant."

"Hello, it's nice to meet you," she said while reaching out to shake my hand. "I hope you like the clothes I picked out for you. I have a few more bags in the car. Dominique, if you don't mind, could you help me with the rest?"

I shook her hand and politely thanked her. I gave that bitch the once-over. She didn't look like a damn assistant, with that tight-ass short dress on and them high-ass red-bottom heels she was wearing. She looked to be around my age, and I wasn't feeling that shit—not one bit. Honestly, I didn't understand why I felt like that. But I knew that if Dominique and I got serious, she could kiss that little assistant job good-bye. In the meantime, I had to finish cooking and let her do her job. I wasn't his woman, so I didn't have any say-so in his shit. Once the food was done, I set the table and placed all of the food on it. When Dominique came back, his little assistant wasn't with him. "Great," I thought to myself, and then I finished setting the table. He walked around the table to where I was standing and wrapped his arms around my waist.

"You know that you don't have shit to worry about when it comes to Ashley, right?" I was confused about why he thought that I was worried about her. I turned around to face him, and before I could speak, he just shook his head.

"I saw the way you looked at her when she came in, Chyna. I don't miss shit. Like I told you the first time I met you, the body speaks before the mouth can even open." I swear, didn't shit get past him.

"Well, I'm not worried, because you're not my man. And even if you were, a nigga's going to do what he wants, no matter what. I learned that the hard way."

I tried to turn around to make sure that I had everything on the table, but he grabbed my arm and turned my ass right back around.

"Don't ever turn your back on me when I'm talking to you, Chyna. And make that the last time that you put me in the same category as that bitch-ass nigga. That's the last time I'm gonna tell you that, shorty. There won't be a third time," he said as he let go of my arm and smacked me on the ass. "Thanks for the food. Shit looks good as hell, ma," he said. Then he just walked to the other side of the table and sat down like everything was fine. I felt like a little kid who just kept getting in trouble. After we ate I went upstairs to get dressed for the day. When I went to look at the clothes she'd picked out for me, I saw that they were all from top designers. I dropped everything when I came across the Chanel bag. I couldn't believe that this nigga had actually bought me a Chanel purse. Hell, fuck the clothes—I would've worn only the bag if I could've.

"So I take it that you like the purse?" I turned around and saw him standing in the doorway, looking at me.

"Yes, I love my bag and the clothes. Thank you." I started to tell him that he didn't have to go out of his way to buy me things, but I decided not to. The last thing I was trying to do was get my ass checked for the third time that day.

"I'm glad that you like everything. Now that you have clothes, get dressed. We got shit to do." He must have read my facial expression, because he added "please" and "thank you" to the end of his instructions.

Cinnamon

It was Saturday night, the night of Choppa's birthday bash, and I had butterflies. I'd known that I would cross roads with Malik, but I hadn't been expecting to feel this way. To make matters worse, I had to go to the party alone because Chyna had gone with Dominique, leaving me to go by myself. As I finished applying my mascara, I gave myself the once-over. I didn't want to overdress, and I didn't want to underdress, so I chose all-black leather pants and a lace see-through shirt with a black blazer to match. My hair had big, loose curls in it that I was sure I was going to sweat out by the end of the night if this party was anything like the last one we'd gone to. Once I'd put on my red Mac lipstick, I headed out the door. On the way to the club, I smoked a blunt to calm my nerves. I couldn't understand how a nigga I'd barely held a conversation with could make me feel the way I was feeling. When I was inside the club, I had to push my way through the crowd of people just to get to the other side of the club. Once I was through the doors to the VIP section, I spotted Chyna, who looked like she was having the time of her life. Just when I was about to walk over to her and tap her on the shoulder, she turned around and walked over to where I was.

"Well, damn, it's about time that you got here. For a minute I thought you weren't gonna come."

"You know I do everything last minute. Where's Choppa? I want to tell him happy birthday."

"Right over there." She pointed to him. He was standing right next to Malik and drinking out of a bottle of Ace. When I got over to where they were, I tapped him on his shoulder to get his attention.

"Happy Birthday, Choppa."

He smiled a little before he spoke. I could tell that he was fucked up by the way he was standing and slurring his words.

"Right on, ma, thank you for coming. There's an open bar and food in the next room. Help yourself, and have fun."

"Thank you, I will." I looked at Malik, who obviously didn't care that he was staring a hole right through me. "Are you just going to stare at me, or are you going to speak?" I said.

He chuckled a little and licked his lips. "You know that mouth of yours is going to get you into a lot of trouble, don't you know?"

"So I've heard. I've made it this far with it, though. I think I'll be just fine."

"Yeah, that's because you've never had a real nigga put you in your place. You're used to those weak niggas who let you run right over them."

I couldn't do shit but laugh. That nigga was full of himself. "Well, I'll let you know when I come across one. In the meantime, there's no filter on the shit I say." With that being said, I walked away to speak to and mingle with the rest of the crowd. It was about two in the morning when they brought out this big-ass cake that looked like if you blew on it, it would fall over. The caked looked so real that you would have never known there were two naked-ass strippers in there. On the count of three, they burst out of the cake and began to give Choppa a lap dance. Once it was over, the three of them went to another room. Only God knew what was about to go down in that room. Once the party was over, I sat and waited for Chyna to gather all of her things. While I waited on her, I read a book through the Kindle app on my phone. That was the thing with me—I loved to read hood love stories. I could read a book within hours if it was good.

"What's so important in that phone? Seems like you can't put it down." I hadn't seen Malik walk up to me, so he kind of caught me off guard.

"Well, if you must know, I'm reading a book." I never took my eyes off of my phone as I spoke to him.

"What's the name of the book you're reading?"

"It's called *A Dangerous Love Story*." I put my phone down and looked him in the eye. "You've got my attention now. What's up?"

Instead of answering my question, he reached down and grabbed my phone. He started punching in numbers, and when he pulled his phone out of his pocket a couple of seconds later, it started ringing. "Did this nigga really just steal my damn number right in front of my face?" I thought to myself.

He handed my phone back to me and said, "I'll call you."

"Wait, how could you just steal my damn number?"

"The same way you just let me take your phone. Look, shorty, you don't have to answer the phone. But like I said, I'm gonna call you." And with that, he walked away, leaving me speechless.

Malik

Seeing Cinnamon again for the first time since my party made me remember why I'd wanted shorty in the first place. But what I couldn't understand was why she acted as if I was nothing—as if she didn't want me as badly as I wanted her. I'd never had to work that hard to keep a bitch's attention. When most bitches see a nigga with some money, they're on his dick like flies on shit. Cinnamon was the type of girl who needed a real nigga in her life. She was used to those niggas who let her say and get away with whatever. Shorty didn't know it yet, but shit was about to change. It'd been a few days since I'd taken her number. I'd been so wrapped up in the streets that I hadn't even given her a call. I had some free time, so I hit her up. On the fourth ring, she answered the phone.

"Hello."

"What's up, ma? How's your day going?"

"Um, let me guess. This must be Mr. Steal Your Number. What's up?"

"I mean, if that's what you want to call it. But, yeah, it's me. Now get dressed. I'm on my way to come get you."

"Excuse me, but are you talking to me or to someone else? Because the last time I checked, I don't take orders from a nigga who's not my man."

I swear, this girl's mouth was out of control. I was going to have to get shorty together quick.

"Who else is on the phone? Look, I'll be there in thirty minutes. Be ready." I hung up before she could say anything else. I wasn't about to argue with shorty. I'd said what I'd said, and that was that. Once I pulled up to her condo, I got out my car and rang the doorbell. Minutes later she came to the door wearing a tank top and some shorts. Her facial expression told me everything that her mouth wasn't saying.

"Are you going to just stand there, looking at me, or are you going to let a nigga in? It's hot as hell out here, shorty." With that being said, she moved to the side and let me in. I walked in and went up the stairs. Once I was upstairs and seated, shorty went off on me.

"First you steal my damn number, and then your black ass pops up at my house like you're running shit. How the hell did you find out where I stay? I never said yes to going anywhere with you, so why are you here?" I let her get everything she had to say out before I spoke.

"Look, shorty—"

"My name is Cinnamon."

"Well, Cinnamon, are you done going off on me? Look, I called you an hour ago and told you to be ready. And as for how I found out where you stay—I mean, come on, now. It doesn't take a rocket scientist to figure that out. Now, if you're done going off on me, go get dressed. I'm hungry. I haven't eaten since this morning." She just stood there for a minute with her arms crossed, looking like she wanted to body bag my ass.

"I hate repeating myself, Cinnamon. You must need some help getting dressed. I don't mind helping you out, ma." She stuck her middle finger up and took off toward the back of the house. I didn't know what type of nigga shorty was used to dealing with, but I wasn't like those other niggas. I sat and waited for about thirty minutes, and then she returned to the living room fully dressed. Cinnamon had a certain kind of beauty. When you looked at her, you couldn't help but stare. I loved the fact that she didn't wear makeup. She was the true definition of beautiful.

"You look beautiful," I said, but her mean little ass just mugged and said thank you. Once we were outside, I opened the car door for her, and we left. Most of the ride was quiet. She just bobbed her head to the music and rapped along to the songs she liked.

"Do you like Ruth Chris?" I asked her

"Yeah, I don't care where we eat as long as we eat."

Chapter Eight

(Cinnamon)
Nothing Like Those
Other Niggas

I was sitting at home watching *Empire* when Malik called me. Truth be told, I wasn't expecting his phone call, since it had been a few days since he'd stolen my number. When his number popped up on my screen, I knew that it was him. I damn near had the first three digits of the numbers given to me memorized. I wasn't big on saving numbers, because I knew I would never use them. But I didn't expect him to pop up at my house. I knew that there was only one person who could've told him where I stayed, and that was Dominique. I couldn't wait to bump into that nigga so that I could tell him about himself.

The whole time I was going off on Malik about his popping up at my house, he never said a word. He just sat on the couch with his hands behind his head, all relaxed and shit like what I was saying didn't matter. After I did all of that talking, his nonchalant ass simply told me to go get dressed. It was like everything I'd said had gone in one ear and out the other. It wasn't what he said that made me get dressed—it was more the tone of his voice and his facial expression that made me believe that if I didn't get dressed, he damn sure wouldn't mind helping me. I knew that

62

the only way to get rid of him was to just play by his rules. Once I got dressed, we headed out the door and were on our way to eat. I would be lying if I said that I wasn't feeling Malik. He had my full attention, and he didn't even know it. Once we arrived at Ruth Chris, the owner came over and greeted him by his name while shaking his hand.

"Malik, my main man. It's good to see you, my friend. When I heard you were coming, I made sure that everything was set up just how you like it."

"Good looking out, Eddie. This is Cinnamon, and, Cinnamon, this is Eddie. We go way back."

"Indeed we do. It's nice to meet you, Ms. Cinnamon. May I say that you are truly beautiful?"

"Thank you, it's nice to meet you as well," I said as I shook the man's hand.

"Ok, now, please follow me. I have a table ready for you two."

Once we were at our table and seated, Malik began to stare at me. I was so happy when the waiter came to take our drink orders. When she returned to the table with our drinks, I wasted no time and started drinking some of my red wine. This man had me feeling some type of way with his cocky-ass attitude and his demanding-ass ways.

"Why do you always stare at me?" I asked him. I had to ask him—shit, I wanted to know the answer.

"I must make you feel unconformable," he said with a smirk on his face. That nigga was the definition of cocky.

"No, you don't make me feel unconformable, but I would love to know why you feel the need to stare at me all of the time."

"Sometimes I stare accidentally because you're that beautiful to me, and other times I stare because I can't seem to figure out how a woman as beautiful as you could be so cold. But I can handle everything that you try to throw at me. You'll see for yourself that I'm nothing like those other niggas."

"Thank you for the compliment, but we'll see about that last part." The waiter returned, and we ordered our food. While we waited for the food to come out, we sat and talked.

"So while I'm here, I have to ask you if you have a woman, a boo, a bae, a baby mama, or just a crazy-ass bitch who thinks that y'all are more than what y'all really are, because I don't have time for drama. I don't care about the hos. I feel that if a man is single, he's free to do what he wants, and hos come with the territory. But I will not fuck with a nigga who has a whole bitch at home."

He took a sip of his Hennessy before he spoke. "To answer your question, no, I don't have a woman or any of that other shit you just mentioned. I'm not going to lie to you—I have bitches who I see from time to time, but I've never been in love. No woman has ever come close to getting my heart. These bitches are on a come up. I'll be damned if I let a nothing-ass bitch make me lose everything I've worked so hard for. I hope that answers your question. So what about you?"

"Trust and believe that if I had a man, I wouldn't be sitting here talking to you. I have something like friends."

"What's your definition of a 'friend'?"

"Someone who is just there to talk to me when I'm bored. I haven't been in a relationship in a year, and I haven't had sex in eight months. Does that answer your question?"

He gave me a look like he didn't believe me. "Why have you been single for so long? Or is that just the way you are, period?"

"Because niggas these days are lame and a bunch of tender dicks. I feel like they're only coo' right after we meet. You don't have to stop doing the shit you were doing before you met me just because we're trying to get to know each other. If shit gets serious, then we'll cross that bridge when we get there. So why try to sell me a dream and pretend like you're not fucking bitches while you're still single? I hate liars. If you can lie to me about something that little, then you can lie to me about anything. Once I catch a nigga in a lie, I cut him off completely. I don't have time for that shit. Does that about sum it up for you?"

"Yeah, it does. Well, I'm not going to lie to you or sell you a dream. That's not the type of nigga I am. I told you what it is—it's your choice to fuck with me or not. But I won't beg you to or look at you differently if you don't." For a moment that seemed to last forever, we just looked at each other.

"Ditto" was all I had to say, and right after I said that, the waitress came to the table with our food. For the rest of the night, we ate, drank, and talked. I can honestly say that I'd judged Malik before I'd ever had a real conversation with him. His mind-set and the conversation we had, had every nigga who'd ever stepped to me beat. I couldn't remember the last time a man had held my attention for that long. It was going on eight o'clock, and I had to be at work the next morning, and I still wanted to finish reading *The Pleasure of Pain*. On the way home, we passed a blunt back and forth while listening to Starlito's *Introversion* mixtape. When the song "Lil' Bit" with

Don Trip came on, I began to rap along with it. I could tell that he hadn't been expecting me to know who Starlito and Don Trip were, let alone every word to that song. He turned the music down and looked at me.

"What you know about them, ma?"

I gave him a funny look. "What you know about them? I've been rocking with them."

"Ah yeah? Go ahead. Let me hear you spit the rest of the song." He turned the music back up, and I rapped along to both of their parts, not missing one word. He began to laugh.

"What's so funny?"

"You."

"Oh, so I'm a comedian now?"

"No, you're just different, but I like that about you."

"I guess I'll take that as a compliment. You're pretty cool yourself, if I must say it."

When we pulled up in front of my condo, he got out of the car, opened my door, and walked me to my front door.

"Thank you for letting me take you out tonight. I really enjoyed getting to know you a little better."

"Well, you didn't leave me much of a choice, now did you? But you're welcome. I'm glad I went out with you. I had a nice time."

He laughed at me. "One day you're gonn' learn to keep that smart mouth of yours closed."

"Well, until that day comes, prepare yourself for whatever comes out of my mouth next," I said as I unlocked my front door.

"Well, in the meantime, keep in contact with me, and I'll do the same," he said.

"Likewise." After we said our good-byes, I walked into the house, jumped in the shower, and began reading my book, which didn't last long. I couldn't stop thinking about Malik.

"What is it about this man that has me in such a daze?" I thought to myself as I lay in bed.

Malik

After dropping Cinnamon off, I headed over to my restaurant to meet up with Dominique and Markese. The whole ride there, I couldn't seem to get her off of my mind. I was really feeling shorty. I'd come across all types of bitches, but I'd never vibed with them the way I'd vibed with her. She was different from the rest—she was a whole different kind of breed. Shorty didn't have to say it, but I could tell that some nigga had fucked her over before. Her whole demeanor yelled "Fuck a nigga," but I planned on changing that. I wanted to show her that a street nigga could take care of her just as good as any other nigga could. But I didn't want to rush shit with her—I knew that in due time, everything would work itself out. When I pulled up to my restaurant, Dominique and Markese were standing outside of their cars, talking. Once I got out of the car, I walked over and gave both of them some dap.

"Wassup, fam?" Markese asked.

"Same shit, different day, fam. Let's count this money and the product. Where are Choppa and Zilla?"

"They should be pulling up with the shipment any minute now."

You see, although I'd opened a restaurant to turn my dirty money clean, I also used it to bring in my drugs and my money. Every time I placed an order for the restaurant, I made sure that it was on a day when one of my shipments would be coming in. All of the money and drugs would be wrapped up and placed in a box under all of the food and supplies. I'd gotten a call earlier saying that some shit had happened and that the driver hadn't been able to deliver my load. So I'd sent Choppa and Zilla to pick that shit up. Fuck waiting—I needed my shit. I ran a multimillion-dollar operation, and I wasn't about to lose money because they didn't have their shit together on their end. I gave Choppa the word to lay muthafuckas down if some shit didn't seem right. I would just have to deal with the outcome later. While we sat and waited for Choppa and Zilla, I grabbed a bottle of Hennessy from behind the bar and poured us some shots.

"Aye, fam, you handle that shit with shorty?"

"Yeah, good looking out for her address too. You know, she went off when I popped up there, so be prepared to hear about it when she sees you."

Dominique started to laugh. "Ah shit, fam. Cinnamon's little ass seems crazy. I'm not trying to beef with shorty."

I couldn't do anything but laugh at him. Just when I was about to roll a blunt, Choppa called to say that he was out back. "Good," I thought. I'd been starting to get worried about my little nigga's. Truth be told, I would've rather lost all of the money and product than lose my little nigga's. When I got to the back door, he was already out of the truck and walking to the door with Zilla right behind him.

"Good looking out, fam," I said while giving him and Zilla some dap at the same time. "Did everything run smoothly when you got there?"

"No problem, and you know that I've got you. And, yeah, everything went as planned. You know me. I had Choppa with me, and I wasn't gonna leave out that bitch without a fight." That's why I fucked with Choppa the way I did—that little nigga was always ready, no matter what.

"I already knew, fam. That muthafucka stays glued to you. Let's get this shit off the truck and bagged up." After we counted all of the money and placed the product in duffel bags to be taken to Brenda's, we sat and chopped it up for about an hour until Markese got a call from one of his hos. I swear, that nigga had fucked more bitches than the law allowed. He was wild with them, not caring if they were friends, family, or enemies— nigga was just ruthless when it came to bitches. Don't get me wrong—I'd done my dirt, but I hadn't done anything like the shit he'd done. Once everyone was gone and I had the place locked up, I jumped in my car and left. It was still a little too early for me to be going home. I had a few text messages from a few little bitches, but I really didn't feel like bothering with them worrisome bitches, so I headed to the strip club.

Cinnamon

It had been two months since the night Malik and I had gone out on our first date, and ever since that night, we'd been seeing a lot of each other. I would be lying if I said that I wasn't head-over-heels crazy about that nigga, and I hadn't even had the dick yet. I could only imagine what kind of state of mind I'd be in then. I loved everything about him, from the way he checked me when I had an attitude to the way he treated me as a woman. I even loved his nonchalant attitude and how he was able to deal with my moody ways. I can honestly say that he balanced me out.

I had just finished getting my nails and toenails done and was waiting for Stonie to finish getting her eyebrows done when two loud-mouthed bitches came walking in. At first I overlooked them, but then I realized that the light-skinned thick one was the same bitch who'd been sitting on Malik's lap the night his club had opened. I watched as the lady told them to have a seat and said that someone would be with them shortly. I gave her the once-over. I'm not a hating-ass bitch. I give props when they're due. She was a pretty red bone, and from the looks of it, she seemed like a bitch who kept herself up. I listened as the bitch went on and on about how she knew she wasn't going anywhere and about how some nigga had never kept a bitch around as long as he'd kept her.

I didn't care to hear any more of their conversation. I was just about to go see what was taking Stonie so long when I heard her friend mention Malik. That alone stopped me in my tracks. Her friend kept saying that she'd lucked up with Malik and that she wished she could have Dominique. I'm not going to stunt—although Malik and I weren't anything but friends, hearing another bitch talk about him the way she was had me hot. I was pissed off, but I had to remind myself that he was single and free to do what he wanted. It would've been different if he'd lied to me, but he hadn't. He'd kept it real, so I couldn't do shit but brush it off and act as if I hadn't heard her. I just knew for sure then that I had to keep a friend or two around.

"Ok, I'm ready," Stonie said, causing me to snap out of my thoughts.

"Well, it's about damn time. Come on. I'm ready to go, bitch. I need to smoke." Once we got to my car, I asked Stonie to drive so that I could roll up a blunt and smoke.

"I know you're not tripping because of those bitches at the nail shop. I heard their conversation. Hell, I think everybody in there heard those loud-mouthed bitches."

"Great," I thought. Leave it up to Stonie to catch everything. I inhaled the kush before I answered her. "I'm not tripping because of that shit. I mean, at first when I heard it, I got mad, but I had to check myself. That nigga doesn't owe me shit. We haven't had sex or kissed or anything, so I can't be mad. And for damn sure, I'm not about to ask him about it. I'm just gonna keep a few friends around to fall back on and remind myself to not get comfortable," I said as I reached over to pass the blunt to Stonie.

"I can understand that, but you know my motto: fuck a nigga, and be about your business." I just shook my head as I grabbed the blunt. Stonie hadn't been the same since her last nigga had done her wrong. I mean, I know I'm not one to judge, but Stonie had been like this for the past three years. I just hoped that she wouldn't miss out on that one man who would be willing to love her unconditionally because she was still stuck on what her last nigga had done to her.

"Since I'm in town for the next week, how about we go out tonight? Where's Chyna's ass? She's been MIA ever since she got with Dominique."

"The last time I talked to her, they were in Miami, but we can still go out. I could use a drink and some fun." For the rest of the day, we did a little shopping, went out to eat, and saw a movie. We had a lot of catching up to do—we hadn't seen each other over the past two months.

It was going on twelve thirty in the morning by the time we were ready to hit the club. I was ready to have some fun and to dance. The dress I'd chosen to wear fit my body like a glove fit a hand. The only thing I was worried about was how short it was—I literally had to pull it down every time I took a step. Once we were in the club, we started taking shots of Patron. I was feeling myself a little too much. I hardly ever dance with niggas, but some fine, tall brown-skinned nigga came up behind me while I was dancing to Future's "Real Sisters." I looked him up and down, said "fuck it," and started dancing. While I bounced my ass to the beat, I could feel his hands on my hips, trying to bring me closer to him.

Dude really had some balls, because he whispered in my ear, "Li'l mama, you're the baddest thing in here. I wouldn't mind sucking on that pussy one time." I couldn't do shit but smile, but that was short-lived. Before I knew it, I felt somebody grab my arm hard. After the way he'd snatched me up, I thought it might have been security, but when I turned around to face him, it was Malik. I had to blink twice just to make sure that it was him. The look on his face made him look like he was ready to body bag my ass.

Markese was right behind him, looking like he was ready for the dude I'd been dancing with to say anything. But instead he just said, "My bad, Malik. I didn't know she was your girl." And then he walked away.

"What type of shit was that?" I thought to myself. "Who the hell is he, and how could he make this nigga just walk away without even saying a word to him?"

"What the fuck are you doing, Cinnamon?" he asked, his voice was so loud that I could hear it over the music.

"What did it look like? I was dancing before you walked over here." Those must've been the wrong words, because he grabbed my arm again and pulled me through the crowd of people and out through the back door. Once we were outside, I saw that his car was parked right next to the door.

"Get in the car—now."

I gave him a look that said, "Nigga, you must be out of your mind."

"I'm not going anywhere with you. I'm not about to just leave Stonie here by herself. And besides, there's no reason for me to leave." I couldn't even finish what I had to say, because he had walked around the car and opened the door.

"Get in the car, or I'm going to put your ass in there. I'm not going to ask you again, Cinnamon." At that moment I knew that it would best for me to get my ass in the car. The tone of his voice and the look on his face said, "Bitch, I'm not bullshitting with you." I couldn't believe this nigga was really making me get in the car, and all because he'd caught me dancing with another nigga. I hadn't raised hell when I'd heard the shit those bitches had been talking about earlier in the nail shop.

Once he'd gotten in the car, he pulled away. The whole ride was quiet and long. Once I realized that we'd been driving for about forty-five minutes, I asked him where was he taking me, but he didn't answer. Instead, he just kept driving like he hadn't heard me. Ten minutes later we were pulling up to a gate. He punched in some numbers and kept driving. The farther we drove, the clearer my view of the house was, and the bigger it looked. I took in the scenery. This house was like some shit you would see on TV. The house was made of bricks and had big-ass windows, and there were cars parked everywhere. I watched as he got out of the car, walked around to my door, and opened it.

He looked at me and said, "Get out of the car." I just sat there, lost in my thoughts. First he'd snatched me up, then he'd made me leave the club, and then when I'd asked him where we were going, he'd ignored me. He had life fucked up if he thought that he was going to keep telling me what the fuck to do.

"I'm not getting out of this car until you tell me where we are."

"We're at my house. Now get out of the car."

Once I was inside the house, I looked around and took it all in. From what I could see, the whole house had marble floors, and there were big chandeliers hanging from the ceiling. He even had a fish tank set into a wall. His house was like some shit on MTV's *Cribs*.

"Look, I need to be getting back home. I just up and left Stonie at the club by herself. Anything could happen to her. So you can either take me home, or I'll call a cab."

He gave me one of his "I don't give a fuck about what you're saying" looks.
"You're staying here tonight. I have a guest room upstairs with every-thing you'll need—clothes and all. I have a little sister, and y'all are about the same size. She never comes over, and everything is brand new. And as for Stonie, Markese will make sure that she gets home safe."

All I could do was shake my head. He had me and life fucked up if he thought that I would stay here.

"Well, I don't want to stay here. I want to go home. You really have some nerve, acting the way you did at the club tonight. I could have easily acted a fool in the nail shop today after hearing your hos gossiping about your ass, but I didn't. I brushed that shit off and kept moving, just like you should have done. It's crazy how you niggas can do whatever y'all want, but as soon as the bitch you're feeling is with another nigga, you want to be in your feelings. Here's a news flash: I'm single, and I'm going to do whatever I want to do. If you have a problem with that, then you should do something about it. I'll find the guest room on my own. Since I know that I'm dealing with a person like you, I know I'm gonna end up staying here anyway."

I didn't give him a chance to respond. I took off toward the stairs. Truthfully, I was pissed off about what he'd done. He should have given me the same respect I'd given him earlier. Once I found the guest room, I ran a bath, lit some candles, and got in. "Fuck him," I thought to myself. And then I let my body soak in the water.

Chapter Nine

(Malik)
Pay Your Dues

I had been out making plays all day when Markese hit me up saying that this nigga named Sam hadn't paid up yet. Sam was one of those niggas who wanted to live that street life but didn't want any type of drama. Fifty thousand dollars wasn't shit to me. Hell, my watch cost more than that, but Sam knew what kind of nigga I was. When you put your word on something, you'd best follow through with it. If a nigga doesn't have shit else, he should have his balls and his word. And right now, it looked like he didn't have either.

I told Markese to grab Choppa and to meet me at Sam's nightclub. I would have brought Zilla along, but baby Zilla was sick, and I felt that he should be at home with his seed. Dominique had taken Chyna to Miami with him, so it was just the three of us, and that was enough for me. Once I pulled up to the club, I rolled around to the back of it. I spotted Choppa and Markese standing outside of their cars, smoking a blunt. I looked over at Choppa, and he had the chopper sitting right next to him. All that little nigga carried was a chopper. He had choppers that I'd never seen before. The nigga had some kind of obsession with them. Once I was out of the car, I walked over and gave them both some dap.

"What's up, fam? Let's make this shit quick. I'm not about to play with this pussy about my money. Get ready to lay every muthafucka in there down if we have to."

"You ain't said nothing but a word, fam. I just got this chopper, and I'm ready to see how this bitch will shoot." Markese grabbed his Glock out of his waistband.

"You know I'm ready, fam. There's one already in the head. Let's get this shit done. I've got some pussy I need to be knee-deep in." With that being said, we walked to the back door, and I grabbed my Glock from the back of my waistband and knocked on the door. As soon as it was open, I took the butt of my gun and knocked the dude upside the head until he fell down. Markese and Choppa took off inside and went upstairs, where Sam's office was. I was right behind them, ready to lay every muthafucka down. Markese wasted no time and kicked in the door to his office. When we got inside, he looked like he'd seen a ghost. Meanwhile, this nigga owed me money, but he was sitting back in his chair getting head without a care in the world.

"Malik, I was just getting ready to call you," he said, stuttering and trying to pull his pants up. The little bitch who'd been sucking his dick looked scared as she sat in the corner behind his desk.

"Sit your bitch ass back down," I said, holding my pistol up to him. "Choppa, grab her, and get her the fuck out of here."

Once I had the bitch out of the room, I sat down and kicked my feet up on his desk. I wasn't there to play a guessing game. I wanted my money, and I wasn't gonna leave without it.

"Where the fuck is my money, Sam? I'm only gonna ask you that once before shit goes left."

"Please, Malik, let me explain. I was going to call you tomorrow with it. I just needed one more day to get all of the money."

I wasn't trying to hear that bullshit he was saying. "Fuck all that, nigga. You had a dead line. Instead of calling me and telling me that, you took it upon yourself to do what the fuck you wanted. Count my money out—now."

"Malik, I don't have it, man." Before he could get another word out, I was up and grabbing him from behind his desk. I hit him a few times with the butt of my pistol, and he started choking and spitting up blood and a few teeth. I looked up at Choppa and Markese, who were standing and waiting to see if a muthafucka was going to come through the door.

"Hey, y'all. Tear this muthafucka up, and if you find any money, count it up till we have what he owes us." On cue, they began to tear his office apart. I watched as he rolled around on the floor in pain. I walked over to his minibar and poured a shot of Hennessy. I walked back over to where he was. "You don't mind if I have a shot of Hennessy, do you?" He didn't say anything. Instead he just lay there with a swollen face. One of his eyes was closed shut, and the other one was half-open.

"Aye, fam, I found a safe." When Markese said that, I grabbed Sam by his shirt and pointed my pistol at him.

"Get the fuck up." It took him a minute to get up. When he stood up, I could tell that he was still in a daze, because he could barely walk or stand. I walked him over to behind his desk, where the safe was built into the floor.

"Nigga, open up the safe, and hurry the fuck up. I don't have all day to sit here. I've got shit to do." For a minute, he acted like he wasn't going to move—that is, until Choppa kicked him in the back of his head. "Muthafucka, you're moving too slow." He reached out with shaking hands and opened the safe. When he opened it up, there was a lot more than the little $50,000 he owed me. I looked down at him and shook my head.

"This whole time, you could have paid me, and all of this could have been avoided." I looked at Choppa and Markese and gave them a head nod, which was my signal for them to beat the shit out of him. Maybe next time he would think twice before he tried to play a muthafucka. While they were beating his ass, I was grabbing all of the money he owed me. There was a little more than $100,000 in the safe, but I only took what belonged to me. I wasn't no thief. I could have easily taken everything, but that's not the type of nigga I am. Once I had all of my money, I told them to stop. Shit, the nigga already looked like he was barely breathing. I knelt down and told him that next time, he wouldn't be so lucky and that if I ever heard that he was around my area, my little niggas would body bag his ass.

When I stood up to leave, for the first time since I'd been there, I looked out the glass window he had in his office that overlooked the whole club. We could see the people in it, but they couldn't see us. I had to do a double take because I saw Cinnamon's ass out on the dance floor, and some nigga was rubbing on her. I'm not going to sit here and stunt—A nigga was beyond heated from the way she was bouncing her ass in that little ass dress she had on. It made me want to body bag both of them. I knew shorty wasn't my bitch, but I'd started to feel a certain way about Cinnamon over the past two months. I'd been spending a lot of time with her, and I was really feeling shorty. She was the only girl I'd been in bed with without fucking. We just lay there and smoked and talked about real-life shit. I'd done my dirt, but seeing another nigga up on her wasn't sitting right with me at all. I handed the bag of money to Choppa.

"Here, Choppa, take this money out to the car. I have to handle something." I tucked my pistol back in my waistband and headed downstairs with Markese right on my heels. Once I got to the dance floor and to where they were, I grabbed shorty. She looked like she'd seen a ghost when I asked her what the fuck she was doing. Her response only pissed me off even more. Shorty had life fucked up. Cinnamon had that "I'm gonna do whatever I want" attitude. I grabbed her arm and walked her out through the back door and to my car. She acted like she didn't want to get in. I had to let her know that I wasn't in the mood for her shit and that if she didn't get her ass in the car, I would put her in there myself. I wasn't up for that bullshit. Once we got to my house and out of the car, she started talking about calling a cab.

Shorty was really on bullshit for real tonight. Ever since the first time we'd gone out, Cinnamon had been cool. But tonight shit was not adding up. Shorty was on some straight bullshit, and I couldn't understand why that was—until she started going on about some bitches she'd run across at the nail shop. That was the last thing I expected to hear. She never gave me a chance to reply—she just walked off toward the guest room. I didn't know who she was talking about. I didn't keep up with those bitches; nor did I give a fuck about them. I'd fucked a lot of bitches in my lifetime, and I still was fucking a few, so it could have been any one of those bitches.

I'd never had to explain myself to a bitch before, so honestly, I didn't know what to say but the truth. I'd kept it real with Cinnamon from the jump, but I could see why shorty was pissed—it was the same reason I'd gotten mad when I'd seen her out on the dance floor with that nigga. I headed upstairs to my room to shower. I thought that maybe by the time I was out and dressed, she would be calm. Once I was out of the shower and dressed, I rolled a blunt and smoked the whole thing to face. Shit, I was higher than a Delta pilot, but considering the kind of smart mouth that Cinnamon had, I thought that I might need to smoke another one just to get through our conversation. I got up and headed down the hall to the guest room. I knocked on the door and waited till she said that I could come in. Once I walked into the room, I saw that she had lit candles and was lying in bed, reading a book on her phone. The light from the candles made her skin look even more beautiful. I walked over and sat on the side of the bed, and I could tell that she had an attitude.

"We need to talk, Cinnamon."

"No, we don't. You don't owe me an explanation about shit, so you can save your breath." She never took her eyes off of her phone. Instead, she just kept reading as if I weren't there, so I reached out and took her phone.

"Look, Cinnamon, you're going to hear me out. Then if you want to keep reading, you can. But until I've said what I have to say, you're going to sit here and listen." To my surprise, she didn't have anything to say. She just sat there with her arms crossed and her face screwed up. "I can't tell you who was speaking about me, but I told you from the jump that I fuck bitches from time to time. I haven't lied to you about shit. I don't lie in bed with these bitches—you're the only girl I lie in bed with. I'm not out there telling these bitches that I love them or making it seem like I do.

"I don't know what you heard in that nail shop, but those bitches were lying, bae. And you're right. I probably shouldn't have acted the way I did tonight, but I did, and I'm not sorry for it. So if you want to be mad about it, you can be. But I am sorry that you had to hear those gossiping-ass bitches saying whatever it was that they said that made you get mad at a nigga the way you are. I really fuck with you, Cinnamon, and I'm not just telling you that because you're mad, because I don't give a fuck about your attitude. I'm telling you that because I actually do care about you, ma."

I was expecting her to have a response, but she didn't. Instead, she got up. And when I saw her in that all-white thong and a T-shirt, my dick got hard as hell.

She walked in between my legs and held my face in her hands and simply said, "Make that the last time I hear what I heard earlier today." And then she started tongue kissing me. At the same time, she reached into my basketball shorts and started to massage my dick.

Cinnamon

I had just gotten in bed and started reading *Tears of a Hustler* when Malik came knocking on the door. I'd known that it would only be a matter of time before he came into my room, and honestly, I didn't care to hear what he had to say. As far as I was concerned, he didn't owe me an explanation about shit. When he came in, I tried to ignore him and continued to read my book, but that was short-lived because he took my phone and made me listen to what he had to say. As I sat and listened to him, all I could think about was fucking the shit out of him. I was tired of playing the waiting game with him.

Once he was done talking, I got out of the bed and walked in between his legs. I wanted him to know that I wasn't mad but that he needed to make sure that what had happened that day in the nail shop never happened again. Once I had my point across, I began to tongue kiss him. At the same time, I put my hand in his basketball shorts and began to massage his dick. I began to suck on his bottom lip as I softy moaned. I could feel my pussy getting wetter and the throbbing getting stronger. I reached under his T-shirt and pulled it over his head. For a minute we just locked eyes and stared at each other. I could tell that he was about to say something, but I stopped him and dropped down to my knees, never breaking eye contact with him.

I pulled down his shorts. It was one thing to feel how big his dick was, but it was another to see it with my own eyes. That nigga must have been every bit of ten inches—and he was thick. Straight up, he had a horse dick. That nigga was walking around with horse power every day. I took my fingers and rubbed the tip of his dick, where the precome was. I licked my lips and began to lick the tip of his dick, where the precome was. I use one hand to stroke his dick and the other hand to rub his balls. As I gave him some long, slow head, I moved my head up and down his dick. I opened my throat to take him in deeper, and I moaned as I moved up and down his dick with my mouth. I moved my tongue around his dick. As I sucked his dick and rubbed his balls, I could hear him groaning and saying, "Shit, bae. Suck that dick."

I let go of his dick, when I felt his hand on the back of my head, I wanted to hit him with "the snake." "The snake" is what I call it when I use nothing but my throat and move it like a snake moves its body. I used my free hand to play with my pearl. I sped up and gave him everything I had. I could tell that he was on the edge of nutting, so I slowed it back down and looked up at him, only to speed it back up again. I wanted to watch him nut, while I sucked him dry, he tried to push my head back, but I wouldn't let him. So when he nutted, I looked him in the eye and swallowed his seed like a pro would have. I could hear him saying "fuck" and "shit" and breathing hard.

I got up, and I could feel how soaked my thong was. I looked down, and that nigga was still hard. Yeah, he had horse power for real. Before I knew it, he was up and pushing me down on the bed, his dick still hanging out and swinging. He reached down and took my thong off. When he felt how wet my pussy was, his facial expression was priceless. He wasted no time and threw my legs on his shoulder. I felt shivers run through my body as he blew on my pearl. I nearly lost it when he started to suck and lick my clitoris. I tried looking down at him, but I ended up throwing my head right back down. "Oh my god, baby" was the only thing I could get out.

He bent my legs all of the way back and began to eat my ass. I swear, a bitch died and saw the light. I didn't know what was going on, but I felt like I had to pee as he licked me from the crack of my ass all the way back to my pearl. "Shit, baby, I have to pee. Please stop," I said. But those words only made him suck and lick me faster. I tried to run, but he held my thighs down to the point that I couldn't have moved if my life had depended on it. I couldn't take it anymore.

"Oh my God, baby. I'm coming. I'm coming, baby." I felt like I'd pissed all over myself, and I couldn't breathe. I thought he would stop once I came, but he didn't—he continued to suck and lick my ass and my pussy. By that time I was crying—I literally had tears in my eyes. I was begging him to stop. My body wouldn't stop shaking, and I couldn't catch my breath. Moments later I was coming again, and that time I felt myself do something I'd never done before—I squirted. "Holy shit," I screamed as my whole body shook. You would've sworn that I was doing the Harlem shake, the way my body was shaking. I was so happy when he stopped. I just lay there, trying to catch my breath and make my body stop shaking. I didn't even need the dick—hell, I'd wanted to go to sleep just after gettin his head.

He stood in between my legs with a smirk on his face. He leaned down and whispered, "You really want me to stop, ma?" I couldn't make my mouth say no, so I just shook my head from side to side. He began to kiss me, and I began to suck my pussy juices off of his lips. He went under my shirt and took it off. I could feel him trying to put the tip of his dick in, but because I hadn't had sex in so long, my pussy was so tight that he had to work it in. I wrapped my legs around his waist and let him work the head in. He must have seen the pain on my face, because he asked me in a whisper if he was hurting me. I shook my head no because I didn't want him to stop. Once he had the whole thing in, he gave me long, slow, deep thrusts. I moaned in his ear and then bit down on his neck. After a few minutes, I was taking the dick and matching his thrusts. I threw my pussy at him.

"God damn," he said, stroking me. He sped up, and every time he thrust in or out of me, I made sure that I matched his thrust.

"Aye, you're taking the dick now, huh? Turn around, and throw me that pussy."

I turned around and got on all fours and arched my back. "Oh shit, baby," I said, moaning. When he slid in from the back, he grabbed me by the waist and started to kill my shit. I began to move my pussy's walls as I threw my ass back.

"Shit, Cinnamon." I looked back at him, and he smacked my ass. That only turned me on more, and I really started to throw my pussy back at him.

"Oh shit, baby. Right there. Please don't stop." He was hitting spots I hadn't known I had. I took my right hand and reached between my legs, and then I started rubbing his balls and looking back at him. Like Boosie said, "It blow ya mind when you got a dime who rub ya nuts when you fuck her from behind. I ain't lyin'." I felt him grab my ass cheeks and spread them apart. I could feel myself getting closer to coming with every thrust.

He leaned down and said, "Go ahead and come on this dick. I can feel that pussy tighten up." He started kissing my neck and slowly stroking me from the back. With every stroke, he hit my G-spot, and I threw my ass back a little faster. I was about to come, and he pulled out and started to eat my pussy from the back. He grabbed my ass cheeks and smacked them as he sucked on my pussy from the back.

"I'm coming. I'm coming. Oh shit, baby, I'm coming." I tried to break free, but he held onto me tight. I came so hard that it threw me flat onto my stomach, leaving me breathless. "We're not done. Come ride this dick," he said while lying flat on the bed. He might not have been done, but I knew for damn sure that one more round would put me in a coma. He lay on the bed with his dick sticking up in the air. I crawled over to the middle of the bed and stood up so that I could sit on his dick. Once I had the whole thing in, I began to ride him slowly while he sucked on my titties and rubbed and squeezed my ass.

"Yeah, ride yo' dick, bae," he said, smacking me on my ass.

"Oh, oh, oh shit." I began to ride him faster.

"Look at me, Cinnamon." For a minute I couldn't look at him, because his dick felt so good to me. He smacked my ass harder. "Look at me." When I looked down at him, he asked, "Whose pussy is this?" I must have taken too long to answer, because he smacked my ass harder than he had the last time.

"Shit. Oh shit, it's yours, baby."

"Nah, shorty, he said, and he smacked my ass twice back to back while he pumped in and out of me fast. I was having a hard time riding him, the way he was fucking me. "I said, whose pussy is it?"

"It's yours. It's yours. Oh shit, baby. It's yours."

"It's daddy's pussy, right?"

"Yes, daddy, it's yours." I felt my pussy tighten up, and I knew that I was getting ready to come again. He sped up, and we both came together. I sat on top of him, trying to catch my breath, my head lying on his shoulder. My whole lower body was still shaking, and I had no control over it. He held onto my waist as I lay there. For a few minutes, we just sat there in silence.

"You know you're mine, right?" I didn't know what to say. I would be lying if I said that I didn't feel the same way, but I just didn't want to end up hurt. Malik seemed like he had good intentions, but I knew that only time would tell.

I didn't want to fuck up the moment, so I simply said, "Ditto."

Stonie
"Oh, oh shit. Right there. You're hitting my spot," I said as I threw my ass back. Every time I did, he was there to catch it and smack it. "Oh shit, daddy. Smack it again, baby—again." That time when he smacked my ass, he grabbed a handful of my hair, and that shit turned me on even more and made me throw my pussy at him harder.

He grabbed the front of my neck, leaned over, and started talking into my ear as he killed my pussy from the back. "You wanted this dick, so take the whole thing. Quit trying to run, ma," he said, and then he bit down and sucked on my neck.

"Oh shit." I nearly lost it when he started biting and sucking on my ass cheeks. I felt my pussy muscles begin to tighten around his dick, and he must have too, because he slowed down and began to give me long, deep strokes, hitting my spot over and over again. I felt my legs getting ready to give out on me, but he grabbed my waist and pulled me all the way down onto his dick while smacking my ass harder than he had all night.

"I told you to stop running and to take this dick. You gonna keep running?" he asked while fucking the shit out of me. I couldn't hold back any longer.

"Oh shit, oh shit. I'm coming. Oh my God, I'm coming" was all I could say. I could feel my juices running down my legs. After a few more strokes, he pulled out and made me deeply arch my back. I hadn't been expecting him to do what he did next. He began to rub my ass cheeks and to spread them apart.

"Damn, ma." I looked back at him. He was licking his lips and looking at my pussy from the back. He began to eat my pussy from the back, and he placed his thumb in my butt. The way he was sucking and licking my pussy made my eyes roll to the back of my head. I moved my ass faster, trying to match his rhythm.

"Oh, baby, don't stop. Oh shit—don't stop." I didn't know where my orgasm was coming from, because I was feeling pleasure both in my ass and in my pussy. I grabbed the sheets on the bed and had one of the biggest orgasms I'd ever had in my life. My screams were so loud that if he'd had any neighbors close by, they all would've heard me. I tried to lie there and catch my breath, but he wouldn't let me.

He smacked me on my ass and said, "Fuck you doing, shorty? This shit ain't over with. This is what you wanted, remember? Now come ride this dick." I could hardly move. All that time, he'd been in control, but I was getting ready to ride that nigga to sleep. I got up and then squatted down on his dick backward so that my ass was facing him and he could get a good look at all of it. I wasted no time and started bouncing on his dick. I rode his shit like a true cowgirl would have.

"Shit, Stonie," he said. When I looked back at him, he was biting down on his lip and holding on to my waist. I made both of my ass cheeks move. Chyna had taught me how to make my ass jump, move, and clap. Chyna could've put any stripper to shame with the way she danced. While I bounced on his dick and made my ass move, he tried to slow me down, but I only sped up. "God damn, ma." I could tell by the way he was holding my waist that he was on the edge of coming, so I hopped off and started deep throating his shit. I was sucking and licking all of my pussy juices off of his dick and balls. I felt his hand running through my hair, and as he held the back of my head, I could hear him groaning and saying "fuck" under his breath.

I sped up and took more and more of him into my mouth until I heard him say "oh shit," but I didn't stop. I kept sucking him even after he came. I continued to suck him dry until I couldn't feel or taste his seed. When I looked up at him, he looked like he was trying to catch his breath. I just smiled to myself. "Payback's a bitch, ain't it?" I thought to myself. I got up and headed to the bathroom to wash my face and rise my mouth out. When I came back to the room, he was sitting on the edge of the bed with his dreads hanging over his face and breaking down some weed.

Truthfully, Markese was the last person I'd thought I'd end up in bed with. After Malik had snatched Cinnamon up, I'd been left with Markese. Let's just say that after a few shots of Patron and a long talk, we ended up fucking. And based on what I'd just experienced, it had been well worth it. I stood in the bathroom doorway ass naked, watching him roll up. When he finally looked up, he had a smirk on his face.

"You're something else, ma—you know that? I ain't never met a bitch who could make my dick spit up off of head." I smiled a little and took that as a compliment.

"Well, there's a first time for everything. Do you have some sweats and a T-shirt I could put on?"

He gave me a funny look and asked me why.

"I'm not going to put my club clothes back on. I can shower when I get back to Cinnamon's house. I just need something to wear home."

His facial expression told me that he hadn't been expecting me to leave, but this was going to be a onetime thing. I wasn't trying to stay over or none of that shit—that's how feelings get involved. Hell, the way he'd just fucked me and eaten my pussy had my head all the way fucked up. I knew it would be best for me to leave. I was expecting him to try to make me stay, but he didn't—he just lit his blunt, walked over to his dresser, and grabbed me a pair of sweats and a T-shirt. Once I was dressed and had all of my things gathered up, I walked over to where he was sitting in a chair, watching *Paid in Full*, and smoking his blunt.

"Are you going to walk me out, or do I have to show myself out?" I asked. He hit the blunt a few times, stood up, and looked down at me.

"Don't let this be the last time I hear from you, shorty."

"Likewise. Now, are you going to walk me to the door? I would like to get home and shower."

Little did he know that would be the last time he'd hear from me. Like Webbie said, "All I need is one night and just a few minutes. I'ma handle that there, and I'm through with it." Hell, he shouldn't have cared. I was sure he did bitches that way all of the time.

Once I was in my car, I pulled away and headed back to Cinnamon's spot. I turned the radio on, and Tupac's "Run Tha Streetz" was playing. I blasted that shit as I cruised the streets of Chicago. I rapped alone with the chick, Storm: "Now me and you was cool. But I ain't the one to play the fool. Can't make no money in bed, so ain't no future fuckin' you. I ain't the bitch to love ya. Can't do a damn thang for you. If you ain't about money, nine times outta ten, I'll ignore you." I bobbed my head to the rest of the song as I drove home. Once I was at Cinnamon's house, I showered, rolled a blunt, and lay in bed, replaying what had just gone down between

Markese and me. I began to get horny all over again. Maybe staying over at his house wouldn't have been a bad idea after all.

"But considering the way he laid the dick, I know deep down that it's best for me to stay away from him," I thought to myself as I hit my blunt and continued to reminisce.

Chapter Ten

(Malik)
Mama Knows Love

Cinnamon's pussy felt like heaven—God, it was so wet and tight that I had to hold back my nut a few times. The way she threw her ass back and then looked back at me with a smile did something to me. Shorty blew my mind when she sucked my dick and swallowed my seed like a pro. It's one thing to have good pussy, but Cinnamon had the best of both. We fucked all night on the bed and in the shower—we even fucked in the kitchen while she was making me breakfast. For the rest of the night, we lay in bed smoking and talking. Cinnamon might've thought that I was playing when I told her that she was mine, but I was dead-ass serious. It wasn't even because of the sex—I'd known from the first time that I'd seen her that I wanted her, and I'd known from the first time we'd gone out that she was going to be mine in due time. The sex just put the icing on the cake.

I lay in bed and watched her sleep peacefully. I'd been up all night wondering how I was going to tell her what I truly did for a living. I'd intended to tell her once I figured out how far we would get, but then last night had happened. I didn't know how she would react when I told her that I was the kingpin of Chicago. The last thing I wanted was for her to hear it from another muthafucka in the streets. It was eight in the morning, and I had no intention to go to sleep, so I got up and headed down to my room to shower and get dressed. Once I was out of the shower and dressed, I walked back down to the guest room. When I walked in, Cinnamon was just getting out of the shower. Water was dripping off of her body, and a towel was wrapped around her. My dick started getting hard all over again as I looked at her. When she turned around, she gave me a look that said, "What the fuck are you staring at?"

"What are you looking at?" she asked with a smile on her face.

"I think you know what I'm looking at, ma."

"Nah, I don't. So why dont you tell me?" she said, dropping the towel to the floor and showing off her perfectly waxed pussy and those perky titties that sat up nice and firm. I hadn't noticed that she had a heart-shaped tattoo around her areola. It looked like her nipple was sitting in the middle of a heart. I walked over to her, pulled her into to my embrace, and looked down at her.

"Now, why you want to go and start some more shit? You're gonna have a nigga laid up in the house for the rest of the week, ma, with the way you've been going."

"I highly doubt that, but we do need to talk about last night, though."

"What about last night?" She had me confused because as far as I was concerned, nothing that had happened needed to be discussed.

She reached down to pick up the towel she'd dropped. "Well, for one, we didn't use one condom, and two, I'm not on any birth control. I wasn't even having sex before you, so there was no reason for me to be on any, and you left your seed's in me. I don't mind working on being together, but I'm not having not one kid no time soon. So if you want to continue having sex, I'ma either get on birth control, or you can get some condoms."

I had to let everything she'd said register in my mind before I spoke. "Look, I'ma make this real clear and quick: as far as I'm concerned, we don't need to work on shit when it comes to our relationship. I told you last night what it is. You were mine the moment you opened up your legs to me, so you can kill all of that bullshit. And as far as buying condoms, you can hang that up too. I use condoms with hos, not with my girl. I'll work on pulling out, but that birth-control shit is out of the window, shorty. All that shit does is fuck up your body, so make that the last time you mention that shit to me. We don't have to have kids right now, but one day you will have my seed. In the meantime, I'm not trying to hear this shit again." I didn't give her a chance to reply. I smacked her ass and then turned to walk out of the room. I had a few plays to make, and the last thing I wanted to do was waste another minute of my day talking about this shit. But before I could make it all of the way out of the room, she stopped me.

"Um, where do you think you're going?"

"I have to go check on a few things at my club and my restaurant."

"What about me? How am I supposed to get home? I mean, did you forget that you snatched me up and made me leave the club with you? What am I going to do—sit here and wait for you to come back?"

There was no wining with this woman—she just had to have something to say.

"Take my Rolls-Royce. I'ma leave the keys on the kitchen table. I'll hit you up later, so have your ass somewhere to be found." On the way to the kitchen, I stopped in my room and took $20,000 out of the safe. I grabbed my car keys and headed downstairs. I set the keys and the money on the table and shot her a text message to tell her to go shopping. I jumped in the Benz and left. I knew the only person who could help me with my situation was my mother, so her house was my first stop. When I pulled up, I spotted my baby sister coming out of the house half-naked and dressed like she was going to the club. I parked my car and hopped out. I could tell by the look on her face that I was the last person she'd been expecting to see.

"Where the fuck do you think you're going with that bullshit on?"

She gave me a look that made it seem like she didn't care about what I was saying. "Malik, don't start with me. I'm twenty-one now, and I can wear whatever I want." I looked at her like she had lost her fucking mind. I had to calm myself down before I laid my hands on her. I'd never hit a woman, but I would hem her ass up.

I walked up and got in her face, causing her to take a few steps back. "Take your ass back in the house and change. You're out here looking like one of those hos in my strip club. What the fuck would I look like if I let my only little sister walk around half-naked? Take your ass back in the house, and put something different on before I fuck around and cause a scene in front of all of these white people. Don't try me, Mariah."

Instead of replying, she stormed off toward the front door and then slammed it right in my face. I didn't give a fuck about her being mad at me. I hadn't told her anything wrong. If a nigga had seen her dressed like that, the first thing he would've thought was that she was trying to fuck. She had to have more respect for herself than that. I gave her and bought her anything she wanted. Mariah was the only girl in the family, so I had to be hard on her. I knew she'd thank me for it later. When I walked in the door, my mother was standing in the walkway with her hands on her hips.

"I see you done made your sister mad again, Malik. Don't you think she's old enough to make her own decisions? How do you expect her to ever learn if you don't let her bump her head a few times?"

"No disrespect, Ma, but I don't give a damn about how old she is. She will always be my little sister. She shouldn't be dressed that way. You and I both know that."

She threw her hands up in the air. "There's no winning with you, is there?"

"Nope. Now give me a hug, Ma. You're all swollen up in the chest like you want to body bag me."

She walked over to me and gave me a tight hug. "That's because you're always bothering my baby."

"She'll be all right. You got some time to talk? I need some advice."

She gave me a funny look and then smiled. "It must be about a girl, because you never come to me for advice unless you truly need it. So what's up, Son? Talk to me," she said while walking to the sitting room.

"It's this girl named Cinnamon who I've been dealing with for a minute. She's different, Ma, but I don't know how to tell her who I really am and what I really do."

"What is it that she thinks you do? A blind man could look at you and tell that you do more than own a few businesses."

"That's really all she knows. I haven't told her that I'm the kingpin of Chicago yet. I don't know how she'll take it."

"Well, I'ma tell it like it is, Son. If she really cares about you the way you care for her—and I know you do, or you wouldn't be here talking to me about her—then she'll accept you for who you truly are. Real love has no boundaries. Never change who you are to satisfy someone else. Just be honest with her, and everything else will fall into place. I'm dying to meet the girl who's captured my son's heart."

"I wouldn't say all that, now."

"Boy, please. That girl has your nose wide open, and you don't even know it," she said, and she began to laugh. I sat there and took in everything my mother had said. I knew that I had no choice but to keep it real with her after talking to my mother awhile. I headed out to check on my traps.

Mariah
Walking outside only to bump into my brother pissed me off. Both of my brothers treated me like I was a child. I had to sneak around to do everything I wanted to do. I was sick of that shit. If all of the gifts, cars, and money came with that, then he could have it all back. I wanted my freedom. Niggas didn't even want to fuck with me because of who my brothers were. I overheard him and my mother talking. "He has some little bitch, and he's feeling great, so maybe he should stay the hell out my business," I thought to myself.

Cinnamon
Waking up that morning with thoughts of the night before on my mind left me blushing—and with a sore monkey. When I rolled over, I found that Malik's side of the bed was empty, so I got up to shower before he came back. The whole time I was in the shower, I couldn't help but think about last night, and that was when it hit me that we hadn't used a condom—not once—and I wasn't on any birth control. I was young, and I wasn't ready for kids. Hell, I didn't even know if I wanted kids.

I had planned to talk to Malik about it, but when I did, everything I said went out the window. He didn't want me on any birth control.

If I hadn't known any better, I would've sworn that nigga was trying to trap me. I wasn't about to argue with him, because it wasn't going to get me anywhere. I had every intention to call my doctor the first thing Monday morning and to set up an appointment to get put on birth control. In the meantime, I got dressed so that I could head to CVS's pharmacy to get the Plan B pill. Once I was dressed, I grabbed my phone and headed downstairs. I saw that I had a few missed calls form Chyna and Stonie and a text message from Malik that read "Go shopping."

I was confused until I kept walking through the kitchen and spotted his car keys on the table next to a stack of money. I looked at the money—there was $20,000 there. I just shook my head, grabbed the car keys, and left—I didn't touch the money. I didn't need it, and truth be told, I couldn't have taken his money if I'd wanted to. Since I'd been in my teens, I'd always done for myself. Nobody had ever given me anything—I had everything I had because I'd worked for it. I didn't know how to take from people, especially not $20,000. Now, I didn't mind taking his car, though. I felt like a boss, pushing his Rolls-Royce Ghost. I threw my shades on, plugged my phone in, and started bumping Monica's "Superman." I sang along with her, and I'm sure I fucked up a few notes, but I didn't care— that's how I was feeling.

"There is no other place that I'd rather be. There is no other face that I'd rather see. The way that you do me is something like a movie. Waking up to you is like waking up to superman." I sang during the whole drive to CVS and played "Superman" on repeat. Once I had my Plan B pill, I took it and headed to my house. I made sure to buy two more just in case. Once I pulled up, I noticed both Chyna's and Stonie's cars parked out front. When I walked in the door, they were both sitting in the living room, watching a recap of *Love & Hip Hop: Atlanta*, and passing a blunt. They both looked up and said, "What's up?"

"Well, well, well. Look who decided she wanted to pop up after being in Miami for a whole week."

She stuck her middle finger up at me as she hit the blunt. "Yeah, I missed you too. I had a ball in Miami. We should take a trip up there just the three of us. I swear y'all would love it."

"I'm sure we would. With the type of glow, you came back with, we know who got some dick."

"You sound like this bitch," she said as she pointed to Stonie.

"Hell, I wasn't the only one who got some dick. Stonie isn't a damn saint herself."

I grabbed the blunt and looked over at Stonie with a confused face. "Who did that evil bitch give some pussy to?" I thought to myself as I hit the blunt.

"Fuck you, Chyna. How're you going to throw me under the bus like that?"

"Bitch, please. Like you weren't gonna tell me."

"Right, so shut the fuck up, and tell us who it was. I've been waiting for you to get here, because she acts like she doesn't want to tell me who it was. She was talking about how she's not about to tell the story twice."

"Well, I'm here, so who was it?" I asked her as I passed her the blunt. She hit it a few times before she started talking.

"It was Markese."

Chyna and I both yelled at the same time.

"Bitch, how did that happen? I wasn't prepared to hear that. As a matter of fact, pass me the blunt back. I can't believe what I'm hearing."

"Who're you telling? I'm having a hard time believing it, and I'm the one who fucked him. I don't know what came over me, y'all. After Malik snatched you up in the club—"

I rolled my eyes when she mentioned that part. "Bitch, you just had to bring that part up, didn't you?"

"I mean; do you want me to tell the story or not?" she asked with a little attitude.

"Carry on."

"Like I was saying, after you got snatched up and left Markese and me there, we went to one of his condos. We were taking shots and smoking, and I was the one who came on to him. What can I say? One thing lead to another, and minutes later, my ass was up in the air, and he was killing my shit. And for what it's worth, I will say that that nigga can lay some dick. Bitch, he had me shaking and speaking in tongues. And when we were finished, I grabbed my shit and left."

"Let me get this right: You just up and left him right after y'all had sex?" Chyna asked.

"No, it wasn't right after—more like twenty minutes later. I wasn't about to stay and lie there with him. Hell, it was already bad enough that he left me dicknotized. I wasn't trying to catch feelings too." I couldn't do anything but laugh at her. Stonie didn't have it all, but I loved her anyway.

"So since you threw me under the bus, let's talk. I know for damn sure that if you were in Miami with Dominique, you gave him some of that pussy. So spill the beans," Stonie said while rolling another blunt.

"Ain't no shame in my game. Hell yeah, I gave it up. I fucked him up and down the beach, on the boat, and in the condo. Hell, I even hit him with some head on the plane."

I just shook my head—my cousins were a mess.

"You bitches need help."

"Girl, please. I'm sure Malik will be up in those guts sooner or later, if he hasn't been already," Chyna said. But little did they know that he'd been deep up in them the night before. But I'd keep that to myself for another day. For the rest of the afternoon, we cooked, smoked, and caught one another up on what had been going on—until Malik called, asking me to meet him back at his house.

He gave me the address and the code to get in. Once I got there, he was nowhere to be found. His house was so damn big that I got lost while trying to find him. He was the only nigga I know who had big-ass fish tanks set into the floor and the walls with big-ass fish in them. Once I got to the end of the hall, I heard noise coming from a room. When I walked into the room, I saw him sitting down, smoking a blunt, and watching *Boyz n the Hood*. He had a whole theater in his house. I walked over to where he was and sat on his lap.

"Hey, baby," I said, and then I gave him a kiss.

"What's up, ma? What have you been doing all day, since I see that you didn't go shopping like I told you to?"

"I went and hung out with Chyna and Stonie, and I didn't go shopping, because you didn't have to leave me that money. I don't need a shopping spree—"

He cut me off. "I left it because I wanted to, not because I had to. When are you going to get it through your head that you're mine? I do for you because I love to, not because I have to. Twenty grand ain't shit to me."

"Well, it may not be shit to you, but it's something to me. I don't know how to take from people. I don't understand why you care that I didn't take it—at least you get to keep your money." His face turned up when I said that.

"Look at me, Cinnamon. Does it look like I'd be hurting over twenty thousand? And I don't get to keep shit—that's your money. I don't care if you don't spend it right away, but it's yours, and that's the end of that." I rolled my eyes because shit was either his way or—hell, his way. There was no winning with him. I'd learned that the first time we'd gone out on a date.

"I need to talk to you about something." His face looked serious—it was like he didn't know how to say what was on his mind. I sure as hell hoped that it wasn't bullshit, because I wasn't up for it.

"Go ahead. Tell me what's on your mind, bae." He took a deep breath and ran his hand across his head.

"What I'm about to tell you should stay between you and me no matter the outcome of our relationship. After I've said what I have to say, you'll have a choice: you can stay with me or not. I'm hoping that you can overlook it and see me as the man I am when I'm with you, not the man the world sees me as. I haven't been all the way honest with you, but I haven't lied to you about shit. I do own a strip club, a restaurant, and a nightclub, but those are just cover-ups for who I really am and what I really do.

"I'm the kingpin of Chicago. I run a multimillion-dollar drug operation. I'm not perfect, and I can't change who I am. I intended to tell you all of this when we became closer, but then last night happened. I wasn't expecting all of that to happen before I told you, so there. I told you what it is. I just hope that you can look past my lifestyle and accept me for me. I'm the same nigga I was when you met me—nothing has changed but your idea of what I truly do to earn my money."

For a few minutes, I just sat there and let everything he had just told me sink in. I couldn't believe that shit—I was fucking a kingpin. I would be lying if I said that I wasn't pissed off. His whole lifestyle was dangerous, and I knew that I could end up fucked up just because a muthafucka wanted to get at him. I wished that he'd told me all of that before we'd gotten this far. I not only had feelings for him, but I'd also opened my legs for him, and I didn't know what to do.

"Why didn't you tell me all of this when we first met?"

"What do you want me to do, Cinnamon? Just walk around telling everybody that I'm a kingpin—a big-time drug lord? I didn't tell you because I didn't trust you, and I wasn't sure how shit between us would go. Look, shorty, if you don't want to be with me, just say it, and we'll cut this shit right now."

"I never said I didn't want to be with you. I'm just concerned about the fact that you're a fucking kingpin. Anybody who wants to get to you could come fuck me up. And as for cutting off what we have—well, if it's that easy for you to up and drop me, then, nigga, so be it," I said as I got up off of his lap and headed for the door. I didn't have time for this shit.

I didn't want to have shit to do with a nigga who could just drop me as if it were nothing. "Fuck him," I thought to myself as I walked through the house looking for the kitchen so that I could find my purse and leave. "He can find a way to get his car, because I'm taking it, and he'd better hope that I give it back," I thought.

"Where the fuck you think you're going?" he asked me. I hadn't even heard him walk into the kitchen.

"I'm going home. I don't have time for this shit. You can come get your car tomorrow, because I'm taking it," I said as I went to reach for the keys. But he grabbed my arm, causing me to drop both my purse and the keys. When my purse hit the floor, everything fell out, including the Plan B pills I'd bought earlier. I'd forgotten to take them out of my purse when I'd gone home. The look he gave me when he saw the pills made him seem like he was ready to body bag my ass. I didn't say shit. Instead, I tried to reach down and pick them up, but he snatched the pills out of my hand.

"Really, Cinnamon? What the fuck is this shit? A Plan B pill? Really, shorty? After I just told your ass this morning not to go and put this shit in your body, you did it anyway."

"No, you said birth control—" Before I could finish talking, he cut me off.

"It's the same fucking thing. So basically, fuck what I have to say. Do you know how many bitches would kill to be in your spot—how many bitches tried to trap me so that they could have my baby? And you go and take pills to kill off my seed's. Damn, shorty."

I felt all of the way disrespected when he mentioned the fact that other bitches would've killed to have my spot. Well, they could have it.

"Since you have so many bitches who're on your dick like flies on shit, please do us both a favor and go cuff one of those desperate-ass bitches. I took the pills because I felt that we should've used a condom. From the jump, we've only been talking for two months. Why would I want to have a baby with a man I barely know? I did us both a favor."

He looked at me for what seemed like a lifetime. "Next time don't open your legs up for a nigga you barely know, shorty."

He mugged one last time before he walked out of the kitchen. A moment later I heard the front door slam shut. I walked over to the mini-bar and grabbed the bottle of Hennessy. Fuck the Patron—I needed a few shots of the "Hen dog." I grabbed a glass and headed upstairs. I thought about going home, but truthfully, I hadn't wanted to leave in the first place. I walked the halls, looking for his room. When I came to two big double doors, I opened them. His room was fit for a king, with a gold, black, and marble headboard and big-ass chandeliers hanging from the ceiling. He even had a big white rug next to the bed. He was on some real Tony Montana shit, with a big-ass tub sitting in the middle of the room and a big-screen TV right in front of it. I ran a bath, rolled a blunt, and got in. I wasn't going to let Malik fuck up my day. I was going to sit there, soak my sore pussy, sip on his Hennessy, and smoke his weed.

Chapter Eleven

(Markese) Mind Blown

I spent most of my day at Brenda's bagging product and counting money to take over to Peaches'. I didn't know why, but I couldn't get Stonie off of my mind. The way she'd fucked a nigga last night had left me in a daze, and it had fucked me up when she'd gotten up to leave right after we'd fucked. Shorty straight did me like a nigga does a bitch, and that shit wasn't sitting right with me. I knew I had my dog-ass ways, but, damn—I hadn't been expecting that. She hadn't even hit a nigga up since. I thought that that bitch just might've been my twin—like, the female version of me or something. I didn't know, but if she ever wanted the dick again, I'd only be a phone call away. I wasn't about to sweat her—I didn't sweat bitches. I had a line of bitches begging me to come drop dick. I looked at the TV screen in the kitchen and then saw that Dominique was walking up to the door. I continued to count the money that was on the table. When he walked into the kitchen, he walked over and gave me some dap.

"What's up, fam? How you been, nigga?"

"You know me—same shit, different day. Still chasing paper and dropping dick in these bitches."

He shook his head. "Boy, you're a fool, fam."

"So I've heard. How was Miami? I heard you took your shorty with you."

"Yeah, I brought her with me, and it was well worth. But you and I both know the real reason I went up there. I just took shorty with me for a short getaway while I took care of business."

"Yeah, did you handle that?"

"You know I did. You don't even have to ask. That nigga's sleeping with the fishes."

"I'm just glad you made it back. I don't know if you heard, but we had to fuck up that nigga Sam the other night over fifty grand that he'd had on him the whole time. I was hoping like hell that he didn't have it so that I could off his bitch ass. I'm telling you now, fam, if I ever catch him riding through the south side, I'm gonna body bag him. I never did like that pussy-ass nigga—not even from the start."

"Damn. I leave for a few days, and shit goes left," he said, rolling a blunt. For the next hour and a half, he helped me count the money on the table and then bag it up. After we were done, we headed out to Malik's strip club. He'd shot me a text earlier saying to meet him there. When we got there, he was sitting in his office, smoking a blunt, and getting a lap dance from two of his strippers. There was money all over the floor, and from the look of it, he was fucked up. We walked over to where he was.

"What's up, fam? I see you're in here doing your thing. You want us to come back?"

"Nah, y'all are straight. They were just about to leave," he said as he smacked one of the girls on the ass. After they'd pick up all of the money and left, we started to go over the weekly income from all three trap houses. Once we were done, we sat and chopped it up for a few hours until Dominque left, and one of my little freaks hit me up. I'd been hoping that Stonie would call, but she didn't, so fuck her. I wasn't about to pass up some new pussy just to dwell over some pussy I'd already had.

Malik

I spent most of my night at my strip club getting lap dances and going over business with Markese and Dominique. I was still pissed off that Cinnamon had taken the day-after pill. It wasn't the fact that she'd taken the pill that made me feel so shitty—it was the fact she'd acted as if I wasn't good enough to be the father of her child. I understood that we hadn't been fucking around for that long, but why open your legs for a nigga who you claim to barely know? I wasn't asking her to have my seed right away—I wanted kids, but I could wait. I simply asked her not to put that bullshit in her body. My nigga Zilla's girl had been on that bullshit for years, and when it came time for them to have a baby, it was hard for her to get pregnant due to all of that damn birth control she'd been on. I had reasons for the things I said and did.

When I looked at the clock, I saw that it was four thirty in the morning. I grabbed my car keys and headed home. When I got home, I noticed that all of my cars were still parked out front. When I got to my bedroom, I saw that Cinnamon was asleep in my bed. If I'd known that she was going to stay, I wouldn't have stayed gone all night, but fuck it—it was what it was. I walked to the bathroom to take a shower. After I got out and got dressed, I got into bed and pulled her in close to me. She had on a thong with no bra or T-shirt. I couldn't have cared less about her being mad. My dick began to get hard as I rubbed on her ass and planted kisses on the back of her neck. I didn't think she would feel it so soon, but she did, and she turned around with a mean mug on her face. She looked like she wanted to slap the shit out of a nigga.

"Why the fuck are you just now coming into the house at five thirty in the morning? Is this what you're going to be doing? You can let me know now so that I can keep it pushing. I keep telling you that I don't have time for this shit." Cinnamon had a mouth on her that would've make a reverend commit a sin and want to body bag her little ass. I wasn't up for that shit—I just wanted to get in those guts and then go to sleep. I'm not the type of nigga who likes to argue. Instead of replying to her, I slipped my hand in between her legs, started to massage her clitoris, and sucked on her earlobe. When she began to let out light moans, I looked down at her.

As she bit down on her bottom lip, I said, "Now, what was that shit you were saying, shorty?" I got in between her legs and pulled her thong off, but she just shook her head back and forth like she hadn't just been talking shit.

"Nah, I want you to keep talking that shit you were just talking, ma."

"Baby, please," she said, but I threw her legs over my shoulder and began to suck and lick the life out of her pussy. I wasn't about to play with Cinnamon's ass—the only way to shut her up was to put her to sleep. I licked in between her ass crack, which caused her body to jerk and her legs to shake. She tried to push my head back, but I knocked her hands off of me and licked her ass faster until she was yelling and calling me "daddy."

"Oh, oh, oh my God, daddy. I'm coming," she yelled, trying to run. I held her thigs tight while I licked up all of her juices. Once I was done, I looked up at her. She was trying to catch her breath. I knelt down and gave her pussy lips one last kiss before telling her to turn around. I wanted her on all fours. I wasn't going to make love to her—I was going to punish that pussy till she begged me to stop, and even then, I wasn't going to. Once she had a deep dip in her back, I went in with no remorse, hitting her spot over and over again and making her take every inch of my dick. She tried to put her hand on my stomach to push me back, but that only made me grab both of her hands and hold them while I killed her shit from the back. I used one hand to hold both of her wrists behind her back and the other hand to smack her ass. All she could do was yell and scream for me to stop, but that shit went in one ear and out the other. But then I slowed it down and gave her long, deep, hard stokes.

"Oh—oh, baby. Please just let my hands go," she said. In between her moans, I just smirked at her and then went back to giving her everything I had. If I'd never been knee-deep in some pussy before, I damn sure was then. I felt her pussy begin to tighten around my dick, and I began to smack her ass harder and harder.

"You going to keep talking shit?" I asked her while smacking her ass and going deeper and deeper into her guts. Her pussy was squirting, and her voice was shaking when she tried to say no. But the answer she'd given me wasn't good enough, so I smacked her ass again and again, causing her to jump.

"No, daddy. No," she screamed as she creamed all over my dick. I smiled to myself as I let go of her hands. Then I leaned over her shoulder to kiss her while still slowly strocking her.

"You going to keep taking those pills?" I asked her, still slowly going in and out of her pussy.

"No, oh no, baby. I promise I won't take them," she said. And for the rest of the night, I made love to her till she couldn't take it anymore and went to sleep.

Cinnamon

I was lying in bed when I heard Malik's black ass walk into the house at five thirty in the morning. I listened as he walked into the bathroom to take a shower. When he came out, he jumped into bed and pulled me close to him like shit was all gravy. I wanted to turn around and knock the wind out of his ass. I didn't know what kind of bitches he'd been dealing with, but that was going to be the last time he ever came into the house at five thirty in the morning. I turned around to let him know that shit wasn't peaches and cream, but he was rubbing my ass, and I could feel his dick getting hard through his basketball shorts. As he rubbed my ass and gave me kisses on the back of my neck, I tried to talk shit about his coming in late, but like every other time, shit didn't go my way.

He shut my ass up quick when he started to eat my pussy. I swear, that nigga had a mouthpiece that only God himself could have blessed him with. The way he ate my pussy made me swear that I'd seen the light and the gates of heaven. I was on a whole other level. He made my body do things and feel a way that no other man ever had. The way he fucked me put me straight to sleep. I was too tired to even get up and shower—I just closed my eyes and went to sleep. When I woke up the next morning, Malik was lying right next to me, watching TV, and smoking a blunt. He looked over at me with a smirk on his face.

"Damn, bae. I thought you were going to sleep all morning. You see what good dick will do to you?"

I stuck my middle finger up at him and rolled over to see what time it was. "Damn," I thought to myself when I looked at the clock and saw that it was eleven thirty in the morning.

"Why did you let me sleep so long?" I asked him.

"What would've been my reason to wake you up? I'm not in a rush to do shit today. Besides, you looked like you were sleeping good, so I let you."

"Ok, well, when I get out of the shower, we're going to have a talk."

The look he gave me said, "Damn—not another talk."

"Yeah, all right" was all he said, and he continued to smoke his blunt. Once I'd brushed my teeth and washed my face, I hopped in the shower and let the water hit my body. I stood underneath the water in a daze. I still couldn't believe that Malik was a kingpin. As bad as I wanted to walk away and be done with him, something inside of me wouldn't allow me to. Over the past few months, I'd grown to really care about him, so walking away would have been hard. I snapped out of my thoughts and handled my business. After I was out of the shower and dressed, I headed out of the bathroom only to find that he wasn't in the room. I walked all through the house until I began to smell food cooking.

I walked into the kitchen, and some bitch was standing over the stove cooking. She looked to be mix or something, and she was kind of older. Just when I was getting ready to walk out of the kitchen to find Malik, he walked in. I took a good look at him and licked my lips. I swear, if that lady hadn't been standing right there, I would've been fucking him all through the kitchen. "That man is fine as hell," I thought to myself.

"What're you looking at?" he asked, walking toward me. But before I could answer him, the lady turn around.

"Breakfast will be ready shortly, Mr. Malik."

"Ok, thank you, Martha. Oh yeah, Martha, this is my girl, Cinnamon. Cinnamon, this is Martha, my housekeeper."

"Nice to meet you, Ms. Cinnamon. If you need anything, please let me know."

"Thank you, and it's nice to meet you as well," I said, looking over at Malik. "Malik, we need to talk," I said, walking toward the living room with him following right behind me. He took a seat on the couch, kicked his feet up, and put his hands behind his head. I swear, that nigga truly had a nonchalant attitude.

"What's up, ma? You wanted to talk, so go ahead—talk." I rolled my eyes while taking a seat next to him.

"We have to talk about what you do for a living. I'm not judging you, but how do I know that if I continue to fuck with you, shit won't happen to me because of who you are and what you do?"

"Look, bae. I can't tell you what will or will not happen, but I can say that as long as you're with me, I'm going to make sure that you're always safe. I have a mother and a little sister, and nothing I've done in the streets has ever gotten back to them. You just have to trust me and believe that as long as you're with me, I'm going to make sure that you're always safe. I've been doing this awhile now, and the way I handle my business and cover my tracks has gotten me this far. I don't want you to up and say 'fuck what we've got,' but if you feel that my lifestyle is too much, then you're more than welcome to walk out the door. No, I don't want you to, but I can't make you stay with me, and I'm damn sure not going to beg you, ma." I sat and listened to everything he had to say. I'd already known that I wasn't going anywhere, but I had to be certain that his lifestyle wouldn't put my life in danger.

"So what about last night? You always come in at that time of the morning? If you want me as your woman, you'd best not let the sun beat you home. Now that I know what you do for a living, I'll expect you to be out late, but don't let the sun beat you, or you can stay wherever the fuck you are." He just looked at me and shook his head.

"Damn, is there ever a day you don't talk shit? I wasn't expecting you to be here when I came home. If I'd known you were going to stay, I would've come back earlier."

"Well, just don't let that shit happen again. And one last thing—" When I said that, he threw his hands up in the air. He was like, "Damn, bae, you have more to say?" I couldn't do anything but laugh at him.

"You know that if you ever cheat on me, I'm going to leave you and never come back, right? I know what kind of nigga you are, and I don't have time to be beefing with bitches over you. I'll simply drop you and keep it pushing." He grabbed me by my arm and pulled me closer to him.

"I'm not worried about you leaving me, shorty, and those bitches were as good as gone when you opened your legs for me. I'm no fool—I know what I got. You just need to understand that your man has had a lot of woman in his lifetime, so those bitches are going to be mad just at the fact that you're mine, and they're not. You just have to rock with me and trust me." Right when he said that, Martha walked into the living room

"Breakfast is ready, Mr. Malik."

"Ok, thank you, Martha." I wasn't going to say shit right then, but sooner or later, he was going to have to get rid of her. I didn't need no bitch cooking and cleaning for my man—that was my job. In the meantime, though, I'd sit back until it was time to speak up. After we ate, we got dressed and left. He didn't tell me where we were going—he only told me to get dressed and to ride with him somewhere. The car ride was about thirty minutes long. We passed by all of these big-ass house that I knew only white people could have stayed in. Every house on the block was big and nice. We came to a house that was all brick with big windows, and the lawn was nice as hell, and there were flowers and plants everywhere.

Once we pulled up to it, I asked him whose house it was, and he simply said, "My mother's." I wished he'd told me that's where we were going. It wasn't that I didn't want to meet her—I just wanted a heads-up so that I could mentally prepare myself to meet his mother. Once he was out of the car, he walked around to my side and opened the door.

"Come on, ma. What're you going to do—sit in the car?"

"No, but why didn't you tell me that we were going to your mother's house?" I said as I got out of the car.

"I didn't feel that I had to. We're here now, so come on," he said as he grabbed my hand and began to walk to the front door. He knocked on the door a few times before someone opened it. This short, pretty dark-skinned woman with long jet-black hair answered the door. I would have taken her to be in her early thirties. She had the same smooth, chocolate skin that Malik had. She stood there with her hand on her hip and a smile on her face.

"Boy, why didn't you use your key?" she said, giving him a hug.

"My bad, Ma. I didn't want to just walk in on you," he said, hugging her back.

"Well, are y'all coming on in? Don't just stand there." When she turned around, I noticed her body. His mama had more ass than Stonie and I had put together. Her whole body looked fit, like she worked out every day. Once we were in the house, she wasted no time. She turned to me and hugged me. "Hello, Cinnamon. I've heard so much about you. I'm Malik's mom, Yvette."

"Hello, Mrs. Yvette. It's nice to meet you as well," I said, hugging her back

"Girl, please. You can call me Mama Yvette. If he brought you to meet me, then I know you're going to be around for a long time. Are y'all hungry? I just started cooking," she said as she walked toward the kitchen. I took a look around her house as we walked to the kitchen. Her house was beautiful on the inside and the outside. It looked like some shit you'd see in a magazine. Once we got to the kitchen, I took a seat at the table and watched her cook. Malik walked off, saying that he had a business call to make. For the next twenty minutes, his mother and I talked as she cooked. Then I heard the front door open and close.

"That must be my daughter," she said, and then she continued to cut up the potatoes. Moments later a dark-skinned five-foot-six young-looking girl walked into the kitchen. She looked to be about twenty or twenty-one and had long jet-black hair that looked like her mother's, but her hair seemed to be longer.

"Hey, Ma, I see your son is here," she said, not seeing me sitting at the table.

"Yeah, he's here, and so is his girlfriend. She's sitting right there." She pointed to me.

"Oh, hey. I didn't see you right there," she said while walking over to me. "I'm Mariah, but you can call me Riah," she said, holding her hand out for me to shake.

"Hey, I'm Cinnamon. Nice to meet you."

"Likewise. I'm glad you're in the picture. Now maybe my brother will be too busy to be in my business all of the time."

"I'll never be too busy to be in your business," Malik said while walking back into the kitchen. She rolled her eyes.

"Do you hear everything?" she said, hugging him.

"Something like that," he said, taking a seat next to me. And for the rest of the day, we stayed at his mom's house while she cooked. He watched sports, and I got to know Mariah more. She seemed cool. I could tell that because of her brothers, she didn't get to do much, but that would change now that I was in the picture.

Chapter Twelve

(Yvette)
Daughter InLaw

When my son Malik called me that morning to say that he was going to bring Cinnamon over to meet me, a part of me got happy. I love all of my kids dearly, but Malik has always been my heart. He reminds me so much of his father and me. The way that he takes care of his family and the hustle that he has within him make him a combination of us. I knew that Cinnamon had to be special for him to even speak to me about her, let alone bring her to meet me. I wanted grandbabies, and I knew that Mariah wasn't going to have one any time soon—and I was sure that if she did, both of my sons would try to kill both her and the baby's father. I knew that my son Markese would never have kids—I didn't think that nigga even had a heart that could love, the way he sat around and had sex with multiple women. That really pissed me off because I'd raised my boys to love and respect women.

I never thought I'd see the day when my son would bring a woman home to meet me. I'd never heard my son speak about love for a woman other than Mariah or me—or about a woman he really liked, for that matter. I'd always known that Malik would be different. From the time his father had left and gone away, he'd always said, "Mommy, I'ma have some money one day. You and Mariah won't ever want for nothing. So don't be sad, because I'm the king of this family now." When my son hit his teens,

I started to hear about him being in the streets. When I would ask him about it, he would say, "Ma, I don't know what you heard, but that's not me." I knew he was lying—at a young age, he had more money than the average Joe. No matter how much I tried to keep him out of the streets or to put him in better schools, he would still hang out in the streets.

Eventually Markese and Dominique joined him and started selling drugs with him. When my older sister was murdered by her ex-husband, I took in my nephew, Dominique, and raised him like he was my own. When he found out that it was his father who'd killed his mother, he stopped talking for a whole year and became extremely coldhearted toward anyone who wasn't family. He would just read books on the human body and take sewing classes. I began to get worried about him, and I wanted to seek help for him. Then when I went into his room one morning, he was reading a book on all of the different types of medication in the world. When I walked in, he stopped reading, and for the first time in a year, he spoke and simply told me that he loved me, and then he went back to reading. I didn't know what to do, but, thank God—I cried that whole day like a baby would have. Dominique might be my nephew, but to me, he's my son. I did for him what I knew my sister would have done for me.

I snapped out of my thoughts when I heard knocks on my front door. When I opened the door, I saw Malik and a really pretty light brown-skinned girl standing next to him. I could see why my son was attracted to her—her skin had a natural, beautiful glow. The name "Cinnamon" complemented her very well. I could tell by the way she spoke when she and my son were talking that she had a backbone too, and I liked that about her. She seemed like she didn't take no shit. She reminded me of how I'd been when I'd gotten with Malik's father. I'd had to demand respect from him.

Malik Jr. was very much like his father when it came to women. It was hard for them to love, but when they did, they loved with their whole hearts. While Malik watched TV and my daughter talked with Cinnamon, I continued to make Sunday dinner. I was hoping that my other two sons would pop up, but to my surprise, they didn't. For the rest of the night, we ate and talked until they left and went home. Once they were gone, I poured a shot of Hennessy and reminisced about the first time I'd met big Malik. Some days I missed him, but most days I just put him in the past. I felt that no matter what, I'd always love him just for giving me my three kids. But the life I had with him was long gone, and there was no amount of money on this earth that could've made me get with him again. I took another shot of Hennessy, kicked my feet up, and watched a movie on Lifetime.

Big Malik, a.k.a. the "Grim Reaper"

For some time, I'd been watching my kids grow up and become successful from a distance. I was very proud of my firstborn son, Malik Jr. Never in a million years would I have thought that my son would follow in my footsteps and become a kingpin. But little did he know that I was the original kingpin of Chicago. Back when I ran the streets of Chicago, I went by the name "Grim Reaper." I never went by my real name. I felt that would only cause problems that I didn't need. Besides, the name "Grim Reaper" fit me. I didn't care who I had to body bag to get to the top—I was on a mission to become rich and to get paid. All I saw were dollar signs—that is, until I took a trip down to Miami to handle some business.

It was just like any other trip—I did what I had to do and headed home. But the last time I was there, I caught a case. The feds had been watching me for some time, and when I went to meet up with my connection right after the drop, the feds came in at full throttle with a SWAT team. I ended up spending the next twenty years of my life in prison for murder, trafficking, and drugs charges. I fought my case from prison for some time. When I first went away, I sent a message to my ex-wife, Yvette, to let her know what was going on, but she gave me the cold shoulder. That shit crushed a nigga.

Yvette was different from every other woman I'd encountered. She was solid, and I never had to question her. She was TTG and ready for whatever with whoever. She would pick up on shit that I wouldn't notice, and she could spot an undercover pig from a mile away. I knew that I had to wife her and make her mine. She knew the kind of life I lived. Once I got locked up, she completely turned her back on me, and so did my kids. I sent them money every month when I first got locked up only for it to be sent back to me shortly after. Then I learned that she'd packed up my kids, moved them to another side of town, changed her number, and divorced me, leaving me in prison to rot.

But little did she or my kids know that the original kingpin was back, and I would be coming for everything I'd left behind. Spending the last twenty years in prison had only given me time to sit and plot my next move. I'd been running my own operation from behind bars down in Miami. I'd made a few million over the past years, but Chicago was home for me, and I wasn't going to ask for the throne back. I was going to take it, and there was no question about it.

"Malik Green, grab all of your belongings, and come with me. You're being released." About fucking time. I'd been sitting in this bitch for twenty years, and I didn't think that I could do another minute. I grabbed all of my shit, turned to my bunkie, and gave him some dap.

"Keep your head up, fam. You know I got you. The moment I get out, I'ma make sure that you're straight in here."

"No doubt. Be safe out there—it's a whole other world out there." I let what he'd said sink in on my way out of my cell. Once we got to the processing part, they handed me all of my shit and the clothes I'd come in with. After I'd changed, she cut my wristband off and walked me to the door.

"You're officially a free man. I don't want to see you back in here," she said.

I gave her a look that said, "Bitch, I never wanted to be in here in the first place." But instead of replying to what she'd said, I walked out the door. As far as I was concerned, I wasn't planning to ever speak to another pig for as long as I lived. Once I got outside, I took in the scenery. It felt good just to be free and able to take in the sun, the clouds, and the trees—it was a blessing for me. Being in twenty-two-hour-a-day lockdown had been hell. I wouldn't have wished that on anyone.

But I had to focus—first things first. I was out, and I needed to count and cop all of the money I'd made in prison. On one of my runs to Miami, I'd met this badass Puerto Rican, white, and black bitch. She was the one who'd been holding me down over the past twenty years, going back and forth with lawyers, and handling my whole drug operation. When I'd first gotten locked up, I'd found out that the bitch was pregnant, so I'd taken that and run with it. Months later she'd had my little girl, who was then twenty and looked just like me.

"So are you going to just stand there, or are you going to give me a hug, papi?"

When I turned around, I saw Susie, who stood at five foot five, had long light-brown hair, and had a fat ass. Just looking at her in that miniskirt had my dick hard, and her deep accent had always turned me on and still does to this day.

"Damn, baby. I didn't see you standing there," I said, pulling her into me and grabbing a handful of her ass at the same time.

"I missed you so much, papi." I could tell that she'd missed me from the way she hugged me and held on tight to me.

"I missed you too. Now where did you park? First things first, we have to put my plan into full effect. I know you want to spend time together, and we will, but we have business to take care of." I would be lying if I said that I didn't want to bend her over and fuck the dog shit out of her, but I had business to handle. If I could go for twenty years without some pussy, I could go for a few more hours. I was free at last, and it was time to wake up the streets of Chicago because the real kingpin was back, and this time, I was there to stay.

Cinnamon

It had been four months since Malik and I had made things official, and I could honestly say that I'd never been happier in my life. Whoever said that a street nigga couldn't love you and treat you like a queen was lying. Malik wasn't like those other niggas—everything about him was different. "I can't wait to get back home to him," I thought to myself as I packed up the rest of the things in my condo. Leave it to Malik to demand that I move in with him. At first I said no, but then I sat and thought about it.

I wasn't no fool—I'd taken all of the money he'd given me and used it to buy my condo from the owner. So if anything ever happened and I needed to up and leave for some odd reason, I'd always have a backup plan. I didn't let him know that, though. I would let him think that he was running shit until I had to show him otherwise. As I packed up the last of my clothes, my phone began to ring, and it was Mariah. Over the past few months, we'd gotten really close. I'd even gotten Malik to get off her back and to let her live a little. No matter how much he tried to shield her from the real world, she would always find a way to do what she wanted to do. It was best to just let her live her life, make mistakes, and learn from them.

"Hello," I said, answering the phone while taking a box to the living room.

"What you up to?"

"Girl, nothing. Just doing some last-minute packing. What you doing?"

"Nothing. I just came from lunch with a friend. I was calling to see if you would come out with me tonight."

"Yeah, I'll go. I could use a drink anyway. You want me to come get you, or are you going to meet me at your brother's house?"

"I'll come get you from his house at around eleven thirty, so be ready."

"Ok, I'll see if Chyna wants to go out too."

"Ok, just let me know."

After I hung up with her, I began to take all of my boxes full of clothes out to my car. Once I had them all loaded in the car, I pulled away and headed to Malik's house. On the way there, I bumped Kevin Gates's "In My Feelings." That was how I'd been feeling those past few months. I rapped along with Gates: "Don't worry, I'm just in my feelings. It's not a bad thing, bae. It's nice to have someone who understands me, bae." I was in a daze as I listened to the song, thinking of Malik at the same time. When I pulled up to the house, I called his phone to let him know that I was outside and that I needed help with the boxes. Moments later he came walking out of the house with a confused look on his face.

"Why do you have all of these damn boxes? You can throw that shit away or give it to somebody else. You have a whole new wardrobe. Have you not taken a look in the closet?"

"No, I haven't had time, but I'm not throwing anything away. How do you know that I'll like the things you picked out for me? "Can you just help me with these damn boxes, or I'll do it myself?" He just shook his head.

"I'll bring all of this shit in. You can go inside and chill." For a minute I started to say no. Knowing this man, I figured that he would throw all of my shit away anyway. He did whatever he wanted to do like that shit was coo'. I gave him one last look before I walked off. When I got into the house, I headed upstairs to see what was in the closet. Once I got to our room, I went straight to my walk-in closet. When I walked into it, my mouth just dropped. I saw red bottoms, Gucci, Jimmy Choo, Givenchy, Vera Wang, Birkin bags, Chanel bags, and a lot of other designers I'd never heard of before. When I went to pull out the drawers, I saw nothing but panties and bras from Victoria's Secret. He really had every color sitting right in front of me. When I went into the bathroom, I saw that he'd given me my own little sit-down spot with a nice big chair and a mirror so that I could to do my hair and makeup. When I opened up the drawers of the table, I saw the Mac lipstick, mascara, and eyeliner that he'd gotten for me.

"So I take it that you like everything I bought you?"

I turned around and saw him staring at me. "Yes, Zaddy. I love everything you got for me, but I know for a fact that you didn't go shopping for all of this stuff on your own."

"Nah, I let my mama do her thang. I just gave her the money and told her to buy whatever she thought you would like." As he was talking, I walked over to him and wrapped my arms around his neck.

"Thank you, baby, for everything. I really do appreciate everything you do for me. Even though you're a pain in my ass, I'm grateful to have you as my man." Once I said that, he gave me a little smirk.

"You know you can go ahead and tell a nigga you love him now. Ain't shit wrong with that, shorty."

I swear, that nigga was full of himself. I just rolled my eyes at him. Truth be told, I did love him, but I wasn't about to tell him that. "Bae, you know you're full of yourself, right?"

"Yeah, all right. You don't have to say it, but I know that you love a nigga. I have some business to take care of at the restaurant. I'll hit you up later, when I'm done," he said, smacking me on the ass. Once he was gone, I went downstairs, poured a glass of wine, and kicked my feet up in the theater room to watch a movie. I didn't have anything to do till later, so I took that time to chill and relax.

Chapter Thirteen

(Dominique) Double Life

I was sitting in my man cave, smoking a blunt, drinking some Hennessy, and listening to Kevin Gates's "One Thing" when Chyna came walking in wearing an all-white see-through robe and some heels. Ever since we'd gotten back from Miami, we'd been rocking with each other hard—so hard that she'd eventually moved to Chicago with me. When I found out that she could dance, she made me put two stripper poles in the house: one in my man cave and one in our room. I watched as she walked around the pole and dropped her robe to show off her all-red bra-and-thong set. Even her thong was see through. I reached into my basketball shorts and grabbed a stack of big faces. Before I'd ever go back to a strip club and waste my money on those hos, I'd make it rain on my bitch.

The way she was bouncing her ass to the beat of the song made my dick hard. I started throwing big faces on her ass. As it bounced, I hit my blunt a few more times, and she took off her bra and thong. And then she was up in the air, swinging around the pole with her pussy out. I motioned for her to come closer to me. I wanted her to sit that pussy on my face. The closer she got, the wetter my mouth got, and the harder my dick became. I lay back and told her to put that pussy on my face. I wasted no time and started sucking on her pearl. I held her ass cheeks in my hand to keep her in place as she rode my face. I heard her moan as she rode my face faster. I used my hands to spread her ass cheeks apart and began to lick her ass.

"Oh, oh, baby. Right there. Oh shit, baby," she said, holding on to my shoulder tight. I stopped and told her to get on all fours. Once she had that dip in her back, I went back to eating her ass and rubbing her clitoris at the same time. I smacked her ass hard every time she tried to run. I could tell by the way she was moaning that she was about to come. I spread her ass cheeks wider and went full throttle, licking and sucking her pussy and then her ass until I felt her legs start to shake. She began to scream my name and to tell me over and over again that she was coming not only from what I was doing to her pussy but also from what I was doing to her asshole. When I knew that she'd had enough and couldn't take it anymore, I turned her over and dropped my basketball shorts. I brought her to the edge of the couch. Once I had her where I wanted her, she wrapped her legs around my waist, and I picked her up. At the same time, I eased my dick in, giving her long, deep strokes. I wanted her to feel and take every inch of this dick. Once I felt her trying to match my thrusts, I went ahead and gave her some real thug passion, and I put her to sleep.

After she fell asleep on the couch, I went upstairs to shower. I had a business meeting to attend, and I was already running late. After I showered and got dressed, I headed back downstairs to let Chyna know that I was leaving and that I'd be back later. When I got to my man cave, she was still asleep. "Fuck it," I thought to myself. I'd just send her a text to let her know. I headed out of the house and jumped in my Benz. I shot Chyna a text and then pulled away, bumping Young Dolph's "Preach," one of the realest songs to ever hit the street. "Keep it real with yo dogs no matter what." If nothing else, keep it real with them. I knew how I felt about Chyna, but these bitches could have you set up or anything, and that was why I hadn't told Chyna everything about me yet. She knew about my life in the streets, but she didn't know the rest of the things that came with it. I trusted her, but not enough to tell her everything. I drove for about forty-five minutes till I came to an abandoned building. I parked my car and went into the building. When I got inside, I spotted my package sitting on a table. I walked over to the box and opened it. Inside of it there was a phone and an envelope. I looked at my watch. She should've been calling any minute. Moments later the phone started to ring.

"Have you looked inside the envelope yet?" she asked me.

"No, I'm opening it now." Once I had opened the envelope, I looked over the papers and the photos that were in it.

"You have a week to get the job done. Can you do it, or do I need to send someone else to get the job done? As you can see, this is different from the rest of the jobs."

"Yeah, I'll have it done within a week."

"Ok, I'll wire half a million dollars to your offshore bank account and will wire the other half once you've completed the task. I'll send for you within a week," she said, and then she hung up. I gathered all of the papers and placed them back inside the envelope and headed out. I had a lot of work to do, and if I was going to get it done within a week, I needed to get on it.

Malik

As I sat and waited for Cinnamon to pull up with her things, I placed a call to a good friend of mine down at Tiffany to let her know that I'd be on my way in to place an order for my girl. I wanted her to have something different that no other bitch had, and I knew just the woman to go to. I felt that she deserved the world because she never asked for shit but my time and for me to not let the sun beat me home. I eventually talked her into moving in with me. It wasn't like she didn't already stay there—she only went home to get clothes. I tried talking her into quitting her job as well, but that shit went left. She damn near cussed a nigga out. She said that she loved her job and that she didn't want to sit around the house all day—she'd rather go to work. I had no choice but to respect that. I didn't want to make her do anything that she truly didn't want to do. Job or no job, I was still going to take care of her. I looked at Cinnamon differently because she was different. How she carried herself as a woman was what made me fall for her in the first place.

I snapped out of my thoughts when I heard my phone ring. It was Cinnamon. She was outside and needed help with boxes. "What fucking boxes?" I thought to myself. I'd thought that she was just going there to get personal shit. When I got outside, I saw that she had a carful of boxes with clothes and shoes in them. I didn't know where she was about to take that shit, because she had a closet full of shit upstairs. Once I got close enough to her, I had to ask her why she'd brought all of that shit when she had a brand-new wardrobe in the house. To my surprise, she didn't know that it was there—she'd never even gone inside her closet.

While she was in the house looking through all of the clothes I'd bought her, I took all of the boxes out of the car and placed them in the garage. She could go through all of that shit on her own time. Once I had everything out of the car, I headed back inside to let her know that I was about to leave. When I got to our room, I watched as she looked through the makeup drawers with a smile on her face. I loved to make her happy. I felt that no matter how street or hood you are, if you have a good woman, you must keep her happy. After I let her know that I was leaving, I left and headed to Tiffany. When I got there, I ran right into Ebony's ghetto, big-mouthed ass. If she was there, she must have come across a nigga with some money, because the bitch didn't work a job. And even if she had worked, she couldn't have afforded the shit in there on her own. I tried my best to walk past the bitch like I hadn't seen her, but that didn't go well.

"Damn, you're going to just walk past me like you don't know no-body?" I had to take a deep breath before answering her. I never had liked that bitch—she talked too much and knew everybody's business.

"What's up, Ebony? I'm in a hurry. I got shit to do, shorty."

"Well, damn. I just wanted to say hi and to see why you haven't been hitting my bitch up. You just up and cut her off. That's kind of fucked up, Malik."

"Is this bitch really questioning me about what the fuck I'm doing?" I thought to myself.

"Look, shorty, it's best for you to leave this conversation where it's at. Tina knew what it was from the jump. I don't know what she told you or had you thinking, but shorty ain't never been shit to me but a fuck. And since you want to be so damn nosy, I dropped your friend before my bitch had to. You act like you're so worried about her, but really you're worried about yourself, shorty. I've been peeped game, and you've been waiting to fuck me and still are. Stop acting like you're so worried about why I cut her off. She needs to be cutting you off, but that's for her to find out."

I didn't give that bitch time to even reply. I left her standing there with her mouth open, looking like she was ready for a dick to fall into it. Fuck that bitch. She'd been trying to fuck me for the longest time. I never told Tina, because I didn't give a fuck about either one of those bitches. I'd been seeing Tina's calls, but I hadn't been answering them. She'd never been my bitch, and I didn't feel that I owed her no explanation about shit. Besides, Cinnamon's ass would've body bagged both of us, and that was the last thing I was trying to let happen. My bitch had some good pussy and gave some fire head. She was a freak and solid as hell, and I wouldn't let that go for a bitch who I'd fucked on the first night and whose name I hadn't been able to remember till the next time she'd sucked my dick.

"Malik, what's up? I knew that that was you follow me. I have some nice pieces picked out for you that I know you will love," Brandy said.

"Good looking out, ma. I appreciate that." As we walked to the back of the store, I looked over, and Ebony's ass was still staring. All I could do was shake my head. "These hos ain't got no home training," I thought to myself. After looking at all of the jewelry she had, I ended up buying Cinnamon some earrings and a necklace, and I had another two pieces made so that she would be the only one with them. After I left Tiffany, I headed to my restaurant to place an order. I had a new shipment coming in—some of the best cocaine to hit the streets of Chicago in a long time.

When I pulled up to the restaurant, it was packed, just like it was every Friday. To avoid the rush of people, I went in through the side door and went straight to my office to place the order for my drop. After I was done setting up the time and the day for my drugs to get there, I called Kim into my office so that I could give her a printout about what the store needed. While I was putting in the last bit of information that she would need, I heard a knock on my door, and it opened.

"Hey, Malik. I didn't see you come in. Amanda said that you wanted me," she said as she walked in and closed the door.

"Yeah, here's a printout about what the store needs. Everything needs to be put in by the end of the night, if you don't mind." I handed her the paper, and she took a quick glance at it.

"Ok, I'll get on it. Do you need anything while you're here?"

"No, thank you. I'm on my way out the door right now, but thank you anyway. Oh, and I've looked over the numbers for the store, and I'm impressed. Here you go." I handed her a white envelope with a bonus check in it. I watch as she opened it and looked at the number on the check.

"Wow, thank you so much, Malik. But you know that you didn't have to do this. I was just doing my job."

"Yeah, and you do your job well. You earned that bonus check. Keep up the good work, and you'll see more of them."

"Thank you again, Malik. You truly are a good man," she said while walking out of the room. I had everything for my business taken care of, so I shot Zilla and Choppa a text and told them to head over to Brenda's house. She was cooking, and I needed a plate—meaning that I needed a count of all of the money we had made for the week. Once that was done, I headed out the door and back home to Cinnamon.

Markese

Watching shorty get out of the shower and get dressed made my dick hard all over again. For the past two months, Stonie and I had been on some friends-with-benefits shit. After the first time we fucked, I didn't hear from her for about a month—until we bumped into each other at Saks Fifth Avenue. Ever since then, we'd been on some low-key-fucking shit. She'd made it clear that she didn't want a relationship and didn't want to be in love. Shit, I felt like I won the lottery when she said that.

Shorty was definitely the female version of me, and we'd click off the top. The only thing that I didn't like was that she would get up and bounce right after we fucked like it was nothing. I told shorty that we didn't have to lie together after in case that was the reason she would up and leave, but she said, "Spending too much time with a person you're fucking is only going to cause y'all to catch feelings." And feelings were the one thing that she wasn't trying to catch. I could understand that. I watched as the towel dropped to the floor, and she walked around the room naked to get her bra and thong out of her bag. I continued to watch as she got dressed.

"You see something you like? You're looking kind of hard," she said, pulling her pants over her thighs. I gave her a little laugh because she knew damn well that I loved everything I saw.

"Now, we both know that I love what I see, ma. So what do you have planned for the day?" I asked her while I rolled a blunt.

"I'm not sure yet. Cinnamon and Chyna don't know I'm in town. I haven't told them I'm here yet. What do you have planned—besides running the streets all night?" Stonie always had a smart-ass comment about my street life. She either needed to accept it or not, but I was tired of hearing about that shit.

"I don't know," I said while hitting the blunt. "But why do we have this talk every time we see each other? You always have to bring up what I do in the streets. I know what type of nigga I am, but I see that you don't."

"I bring it up because every time I talk to you, that's what you're doing—running the streets. So excuse the fuck out of me for thinking that that's what you're about to do," she said as she walked over, took my blunt out of my hand, and began to hit it. I couldn't do shit but laugh as she sat on the bed and smoked the blunt.

"So I take it that you're not going to up and leave this time?"

"Do you want me to leave?" she asked, looking through the channels on TV.

"Nah, I don't. But while you're here, you can retwist a nigga's dreads and braid them for me."

She gave me a look that said, "Nigga, what the fuck do I look like?"

"Your hair looks fine to me. Just because I do hair doesn't mean that I want to do yours or that I will, but since I don't have shit else better to do and I have a little time to spare, I guess I can. But that's going to cost you," she said while passing me the blunt.

"I got you, shorty. How much you want to do my shit?" I said as I pulled out a stack of money.

"It's not about the money. What I want is for you to bless me with some of that head of yours." When she said that, I laughed harder than I had in a long time. Stonie didn't have a filter and didn't care what came out of her mouth, but I liked that about her.

"You get that anyway, shorty."

"Yeah, but this time, we're doing it my way," she said, and then she winked at me. For the next few hours, we smoked, ate, and watched *Belly* while she did my hair.

Chapter Fourteen

(Mariah)
Freedom at Last

I gave myself the once-over before I headed out the door to go get Cinnamon so that we could go out. I'd grown to really like Cinnamon. I thought she was good for my brother. She didn't let him run over her or me, for that matter. Before she'd come into the picture, I wouldn't have been caught dead in the club. My brothers had always treated me like a child because I'm the only girl—even my cousin Dominique, who I think of as my brother, not my cousin, had been the same way. They were hard on me my whole life, but they bought me the world, so I overlooked the things that I couldn't do. But then I got older, and I didn't care about the nice cars, clothes, or money. I wanted freedom. I had to sneak around to do everything, and even then, sometimes they would find out.

I grabbed my car keys and headed out the door. Once I was inside my Audi, I pulled away and headed to my brother's house to get Cinnamon. When I pulled up, I punched in his code and waited for the gates to open. Once I was close to the house, I got out and knocked on the front door. I was hoping that Cinnamon would open the door so that we could just jump in the car and leave, but Malik answered the door. He looked me up and down as he held the door wide open for me.

"You look nice, Sis." I hadn't been expecting to hear that. I just knew that I was about to hear a speech on what I'd better not do at the club.

I gave him a funny look and then said, "Thank you."

"Why are you looking at me like that?" he said, and then he sipped some Hennessy.

"I'm just wondering why you're being so nice—that's all."

"Look, Mariah. I know you're getting older, and I don't want to fuck up our relationship by trying to control you. I see the way you get mad when I'm all up in your business. I do it because you're my only sister, and I love you, not because I don't want you to have fun. I know what the streets of Chi can do to you. You're beautiful and smart, and you got your shit together. I just don't want no nigga taking advantage of you or trying to get over on you—that's all. I'm not saying I won't get on your ass about certain shit, but I will back off a little and let you live your own life"

Hearing my brother say everything he'd said made me want cry. I never in a million years would've thought that I'd see the day when my brother would let me live my own life, so hearing him say that made my night.

I walked up to him and hugged him. "Thank you, that meant a lot to me. I just want to have fun—I'm only twenty-one, and I've yet to do anything I've wanted to do. And as for men—well, you don't have to worry about that. Your baby sister is still a virgin." I could tell by his facial expression that he didn't want to hear that.

"Yeah, I didn't need to hear all that, but that's good to know. Keep it that way." Right when he said that, Cinnamon came walking into the living room.

"My bad, Riah. I had to recurl my hair," she said, looking over at my brother with a weird look on her face. But he just blew her a kiss and winked at her.

"These two," I thought to myself. "You coo', sis. You ready to go? It's already twelve thirty."

"Yeah, I'm ready. I'll see you in a few hours, Zaddy," she said before giving him a kiss and a hug. Once we were outside and in the car, she pulled an already-rolled blunt out of her purse and lit it. "Let the night begin," she said before hitting the blunt. During the whole drive to the club, we bumped Gucci's *Trap House 3*.

"That album will never get old to me," I thought to myself as I hit the blunt.

Cinnamon

Waking up that morning and then throwing up left me weak as hell and on the bathroom floor. I must have had way too many shots of Patron the night before. I felt weak and tired, and my whole body felt heavy. All I wanted to do was get in bed and go back to sleep. After the night I had, that didn't seem like a bad idea. Mariah and I had a ball. I was happy that Malik had said that he wouldn't trip about her going out with me. Of course, at first he wasn't having that shit, but after I talked to him and hit him with some fire head, he reconsidered.

When I came home from the club, he was up in bed watching TV and smoking a blunt. After I showered, I got in bed ass naked. I was drunk and horny. I wasted no time. I jumped on his dick and rode it all night. We fucked until the sun came up, and I went to sleep shortly after that. He got up and left. I really wished he hadn't, though, because I couldn't move. I needed to shower, but my body was weak. After lying on the bathroom floor for another twenty minutes, I managed to get up and get back in bed. When I went to sleep, it was eleven thirty in the morning, and when I woke up, it was six forty-five in the afternoon. I couldn't believe I'd slept that long. I grabbed my phone to see if I had any missed calls. I had a few from Mariah and Stonie, and I saw that Malik had been calling, so I called him back.

"What's up?" he answered.

"Hey, bae. I see you've been calling. I've been asleep."

"Yeah, I know. I came back to the house around two, and you were still asleep. Let me find out that you're carrying a nigga's seed and not telling me. The way you've been sleeping and shit has got me wondering." It had never crossed my mind that I could be pregnant. I'd just had a period last month. I couldn't have possibly been pregnant. I blamed me being sick this morning on all of the alcohol from the night before.

"I was just tired from going out and getting dicked down all last night and this morning. Believe me, I doubt that I'm knocked up, but when are you coming home?"

"Uh-huh, I hear you. Only time will tell, though. But I won't be home till later. I have a lot of shit to do. I left you some money. You and Mariah can go shopping or something. I promise that I'ma make it home before the sun."

I took a deep breath and rolled my eyes. "Ok, I'll see you tonight. Be safe."

"Always."

Once I'd hung up the phone, I looked at the calendar. There was only one more day left in the month. My heart begin to race. I hadn't had a period that whole month. The last time I had a period had been last month, on the sixth. I hadn't gotten one this month. I jumped up and ran to the bathroom to shower. Once I was out of the shower, I threw on a Nike jumpsuit with some matching Nike shoes, put my hair in a high ponytail, and headed out the door. I was headed to CVS to get a pregnancy test. When I got to the store, I went straight to the aisle where the tests were. I grabbed two First Response tests and headed back home.

I was nervous and scared at the same time. After sitting for a few minutes, I finally got the balls to go pee on the stick. I sat and waited for the result, and after about a minute or so, I picked up the stick and almost passed out. There were two dark-ass lines on it. They were as clear as day. I was indeed pregnant. I couldn't believe this shit. "When did this happen?" was all I could think to myself. I was in such a state of denial that I drove to the hospital where I worked and had them do a blood test, only for it to show that I was pregnant. I was eight weeks along—that part was what fucked me up the most. I'd just had a period last month, but she told me that some women's bodies work differently. What I'd thought was a period had actually been my baby attaching itself to me. She gave me an ultrasound to make sure that everything was ok and told me to follow up with my ob-gyn the following week.

When I got back home, I sat for hours just looking at the picture of my baby that she'd printed out for me. It wasn't that I didn't want it—I just felt like we hadn't been together long enough to have a child together. Deep down I knew that I was in love with Malik. I just felt like everything had happened so fast. I wasn't ready to be a mom. I sat and took everything in. I needed time to let everything that had happened sink in. In the meantime, I was going to keep this pregnancy a secret until I knew just how I was going to tell him.

Chyna

When I woke up this morning, I planned to spend the day with my man. He had been working hard, and I wanted to do something nice for him, so I got dressed to dance for him. When I got to his man cave, he was sitting on the couch, smoking a blunt, and listening to Kevin Gates. When Dominique had found out that I could dance, I'd made him put up stripper poles in the house so that I could dance for him whenever I felt that I wanted to or when he wanted me to. Not even ten minutes into my dance, I was sitting on his face getting my pussy and my ass eaten. All I could remember was lying next to him before I went to sleep, but when I woke up, he was gone. I knew that he probably had business to take care of, and the text he sent me said that he would be back soon.

I spent the whole day cooking him a big meal, laying red and white rose petals all around the house, and lighting candles. He needed to relax for just one day, but as time went by and the afternoon turned into night, that nigga still wasn't home, and he hadn't answered one of my calls. I sat up all night till the wee hours of the morning waiting for him to get home. When he finally walked through the door, it was well past seven in the morning, and I was pissed. I wanted to body bag that nigga. He had life fucked up, walking into this bitch like he got it like that.

The look on his face said it all—he hadn't been expecting me to wait for him. I just looked his ass up and down. I really felt like beating his ass, but silence is the key, and payback is a bitch. I didn't say two words to him. I got off of the couch and went to the guest room. My attitude was on ten, and the fact that he had not one word to say made me even more pissed. I grabbed a Swisher, broke it down, and rolled up a blunt. I'd been up all night worried about this nigga, and he'd just walked in like he was some fucking king. "Yeah, ok. We'll see about that," I thought to myself as I hit the blunt a few times. "Yeah, payback's a bitch, and I'm her best friend."

Chapter Fifteen

(Malik) Taking Care Of HomeFront

Ever since I'd gotten this new shipment in, it had been selling like crazy. It was some of the best dope I'd seen in a long time. I'd been in the streets more this past week than I had in a while, and I hadn't been spending that much time with Cinnamon. I didn't want her to feel like I was neglecting her or putting the streets before her. If she had been any other bitch, I wouldn't have cared, but I rocked with Cinnamon hard. She was my girl, and I didn't want her to feel like her nigga didn't care about her. I sat and watched her sleep before I got dressed. I had a whole day planned for my girl—she deserved it.

She brought out the best in me and overlooked the shit I did in the streets. She didn't bitch or complain about shit, and she always had posi-tive shit to say when I was in a bad mood or going through some shit in the streets. Yeah, a nigga was in love—I'd be lying if I said that I wasn't. Cinnamon had made this thug-ass street nigga fall hard for her. After I got dressed, I wrote her a letter and set a rose next to it before I left the house. I had a few plays to make. As I cruised the streets of Chicago, I bumped Young Dolph's "Cold World" and smoked my blunt. This world was cold, and the streets were full of snakes. You couldn't trust a soul.

I thought I'd have maybe three more years in the streets. I wanted a family, and I didn't want to still be knee-deep in the streets or moving blow in and out of the city. But for a nigga, leaving the streets is easier said than done. A crackhead has a better chance of going cold turkey than a kingpin has of getting out of the game. I continued to hit my blunt as I pulled up to Tiffany. I had to pick up the order I had placed for her. After I left Tiffany, I went to take care of some last-minute shit.

Cinnamon

Waking up to the sound of an alarm going off made me think that I was dreaming. I didn't remember setting one before I'd gone to sleep. When I rolled over, I felt that the other side of the bed was empty. "Great," I thought to myself. Malik was gone again. This past week, I hadn't been mad that he'd been gone, because every morning since I'd found out that I was pregnant, I'd gotten sick, and I'd yet to tell him that I was pregnant. Then the first morning I wasn't sick, my man was not there, so I was a little pissed. I sat up in bed. After cutting the alarm clock off, I looked to my left. There was a red rose and a letter sitting next to it. I picked up the letter and read it: "If the alarm woke you, then you've been asleep for too long. Follow the directions I left for you, and do not call me asking questions, because I won't answer the phone. Just trust me, baby. I'll see you soon."

After reading the letter, I just sat and smiled. "What is this man up to?" I thought to myself. I had an hour and a half to shower, get dressed, and get to the location he'd told me to go to. After I got out of the shower and got dressed, I did my hair and threw some lipstick on. For the past week, I hadn't even thought about getting dressed. I'd come straight home from work, showered, and gone to sleep, so I was looking forward to this day. Once I was fully dressed and ready to go, I grabbed the letter and headed out the door. I got in his Porsche and drove away. I knew that he would kill me when he found out that I was driving his favorite car, but, oh well. When I pulled up to the address on the letter, I saw that it was a spa. I parked the car and headed inside. For a moment I thought that it was closed, because no one was there. But I knew that it couldn't be closed, because it was the best spa in Chicago, and it stayed busy. Just when I was about to pull my phone out and call him, a woman walked up to me and greeted me.

"Hello, Mrs. Green. Your husband wanted me to give you these," she said, handing me a dozen red roses.

"Thank you," I said with a smile on my face. "Is my husband here by any chance?"

"No, but he told me to take good care of you. He rented the whole spa out just for you. He also told me to tell you that this is your day, and he wants you to enjoy it. If I may say so, Mrs. Green, you have a wonderful husband. Follow me. I will see to it that you are well taken care of." All I could do was smile. He was so unpredictable.

"Yeah, he's pretty unpredictable," I said as I followed her to the back of the spa. Over the next three hours, I got a full-body massage, a facial, a manicure, and a pedicure. They even brought out all kinds of desserts and some champagne, which I didn't drink, due to the baby. I wanted to call my man and tell him to get his ass home so that I could make love to him all day and night and tell him just how much I loved him. But I knew he wouldn't answer my calls, so I just had to go with the flow.

After I was done with everything, the same woman who had handed me the flowers gave me a letter from Malik that read, "I hope you enjoyed your day at the spa. You're not done yet. Follow these directions. I'll see you soon." I thanked the woman for everything and headed to my next destination. As I drove to the next location, I was in a daze. I couldn't believe that in less than eight months, I'd manage to fall in love and become a mother. Just the week before, I'd been pissed about becoming a mother, but there I was. I had a man who treated me like a queen, and I never had to second-guess shit. Since we'd been together, everything had been like a hood fairy tale.

"I wonder how he's going to react when he finds out that we have a baby on the way," I thought to myself as I pulled up to the best Dominican hair salon in the Chi. And just like It had been in the spa, I was the only one there.

"How are you, Mrs. Green? Your husband left this here for you. We will take good care of you. Please follow me," she said while handing me a Tiffany bag. The woman had a deep accent when she spoke. I waited until she was done washing my hair to open the bag. Inside the bag were two boxes. In one of the boxes, there was a white-gold bracelet, and the other box had a matching necklace to go along with it. I had a lot of jewelry at home, but those were by far my favorite already.

Once she was done with my hair, she handed me another letter that simply read, "Go home." After thanking the woman for everything, I sped home to see my man, only to get home and find that he wasn't there. When I got to our bedroom, there was an all-black Vera Wang dress with some red bottoms lying next to it and another letter that read, "Meet me at nine at this address. I'll be waiting for you at the door." After reading his letter, I went to run a bath. It was already seven thirty—I had to get ready. While sitting in the tub, I listened to Jennifer Hudson's "If This Isn't Love" and thought of my man.

Malik

I was headed to Brenda's house to meet up with Markese, Choppa, Dominique, and Zilla. We had some last-minute business to handle before I had to meet Cinnamon. When I pulled up, I saw that they were all already there. That was good because I didn't have a lot of time to be sitting around. I still had to meet Cinnamon and get dressed for our date. When

I walked into my trap, they were all in the living room. Zilla and Choppa were shooting dice, and Markese and Dominique were smoking a blunt and watching them. I walked around and gave them all some dap before telling them why they were there.

"All right, fam. I called y'all here because of that last shipment we just got. I'm sure that y'all know by the numbers that it's selling fast. We have a new shipment coming in tonight. I know that I normally don't bring them in back to back like that, but I'm going to take advantage of this while I can just to be on the safe side. I don't want to run out and then have to wait to place an order. Everybody knows which side of town they're running, so y'all need to get with the little niggas who y'all have on the block and let them know to apply some pressure in the streets.

"Before I leave, y'all need to come and grab a duffel bag out of the car. There's an extra hundred grand in each of the bags. If this shit keeps selling the way it has been, y'all are going to see a lot more of that. Dominique, I need you to do me a favor and check out this nigga named Meech for me. He's been trying to cop a shitload of product. I've never heard of this nigga, and I damn sure don't trust him. Something about that nigga don't seem right. He to press to cop this shit off of me. I want to know everything about this nigga before I do any business with him."

"I got you. Give me a day or two, and I'll know everything that you need to know about that nigga." That was what I liked about Dominique—that nigga could find out anything about anybody. Shit, for the right price, that nigga could've gotten Saddam Hussein if he wasn't already dead.

"Ok, last but not least," I said, reaching into my pocket. I pulled out a small box and opened it. Inside of it was a white-gold seven-karat ring for Cinnamon.

"Get the fuck out of here," Markese said while jumping up and grabbing the box so that he could look at the ring. "Nigga, is you for real right now? What's Cinnamon's little ass done to my brother?" I couldn't do anything but laugh. I should've expected Markese to act like that.

"Yeah, I'ma ask her to marry me tonight."

"That what's up! Congratulations," Dominique said, standing up to give me some dap. Right after he did, Zilla and Choppa did too.

"Congratulations, big bro. I still can't believe that Mr. One Pussy Ain't Enough for Me is about to ask a woman to be his wife. This shit is unbelievable to me," Markese said.

I laughed at his comment. "Yeah, I'm hanging up my jersey. Cinnamon's real solid, and I love the fact that she sees past the money and don't take no shit. I'd be a fool not to wife her."

"Yeah, I feel that. I can respect that because my bitch's solid and loyal, and she stayed with me through all of my bullshit. Now we have a son. I'm just trying do right by my shorty, but I just can't see myself getting married right now," Zilla said.

"Hell, nah. I'm not getting married. Y'all see the scratch marks on my neck?" Choppa said while turning his head to the side. "Man, Brittany's ass is crazy. If I married that bitch, the first time I make her mad, she'd try to kill a nigga in his sleep and take all of the insurance money. Hell, nah. I love my bitch. I can't lie—she's real as hell. But it will be a cold day in hell before I marry her ass. We're going to have to get her evaluated first."

By that time all of us were laughing because everybody in the room knew Choppa and Brittany's history. Their relationship was like Ike and

Tina's—but Brittany was Ike because she put her hands on Choppa every time she caught him cheating. But I can say that the love between them was real—everybody loves and does shit differently.

"Hell, yeah. She ain't even your wife now, and she'd kill you in your sleep," I said before hitting the blunt Markese had rolled.

"Y'all talking about sleep? I ain't had no sleep. Chyna's got a nigga sleeping with one eye open."

Markese burst out laughing. "Nigga, what'd you do? I never thought I'd see the day when somebody had you losing sleep," Markese said, laughing.

Dominique shook his head and started to laugh. "Man, I came in the house last week at seven in the morning. Nigga, she was on the couch waiting for a nigga. Y'all know me—no shit shakes me. But I swear, Chyna's got a nigga losing sleep." We all started laughing because Dominique was the heartless one. The fact that somebody—especially a woman—had him shaken up was funny as hell to us.

"Y'all niggas are laughing and shit, but I'm dead-ass serious. She ain't been talking to me, and if she does, it's real short. I've been buying her shit and breaking bread, and she hasn't even touched the shit. Crazy thing about it is that I'm not cheating on my bitch—I just haven't told her everything about my life or why I'm out so late. I know she's up to something. She's too quiet, and she has yet to ask me why I came in that late. She ain't even brought that shit up, yet she has a nigga is tiptoeing around her. I don't know when she's going spaz, fam."

"Damn, fam. At least I know when my bitch is on some bullshit. Your girl's on that let-him-forget-then-fuck-him-up shit," Choppa said.

"Hell, yeah," I said. "I'm not trying to see what Cinnamon's bad side is like no time soon. Hell, her good side ain't too damn friendly. I can only imagine what it'd be like if I were out here fucking around on her. Shorty already made it clear that she ain't going for none of that shit."

"Yeah, Cinnamon's a mean-ass little woman, fam, but she's cool as a fan at the same time," Markese said. For the next thirty minutes, we sat and finished our conversation. Then I saw that it was getting closer to the time when I had to meet Cinnamon.

"All right, y'all. I have to get out of here," I said, standing up to get ready to go.

"Shit, I'm out too," Dominique said. "I'm about to go see if Chyna's still in that fucked-up mood of hers. Shit, a nigga needs some pussy."

"I feel you, fam. I was supposed to be knee-deep in some pussy two hours ago," Markese said.

"That ain't nothing new," Choppa said.

"Aye, don't forget that I've got that money in my trunk. Y'all come get that shit out before I leave." After they grabbed their bags of money, I pulled away and went to meet Cinnamon at the Pin House.

Chapter Sixteen

(Chyna) Payback

I'd been on a rampage ever since Dominique had walked into our house at seven in the morning. He'd been buying me shit left and right, trying to make up for it. If that nigga didn't already know it, he was going to learn real quick that materialistic shit didn't mean nothing to me. What pissed me off the most was that he had yet to even come to me with the reason that he'd walked his ass into our house at that time of the morning. I wasn't going to ask him, though, because I didn't feel like I should have had to. He was the one in the wrong—not me. All day he'd been calling and texting me, but I hadn't answered any of his calls. Two could play that game. I was not one to play games, but that nigga was acting like King Tut or some shit—like he was just so comfortable that he could do whatever he wanted to do. I was about to show him just why he should never get comfortable.

I went and rented out a hotel room for the night. I planned to spend the whole night there and to go home in the late afternoon like nothing had happened. I wanted him to see how it felt to stay up all night worried sick over a person only to find out later that person was ok. I didn't have a feeling that he was cheating on me, and I never would've cheated on him. I loved my man and all of the fucked-up ways that came with him, but I would not be ran over by no nigga again. As I lay across the bed ass naked, I looked through my phone and saw that I had missed calls from

Dominique. I looked at his text message. It read, "Answer your phone." I opened it to let him know that I had read it and then turned my phone off. I reached into my purse and grabbed a Swisher and my weed. Once I had rolled my blunt and lit it, I hit it a few times and looked through the channels on the TV.

"Let the night begin," I thought to myself as I hit the blunt again.

Dominique

During the whole ride home from Brenda's, I tried to come up with a way to get Chyna out of her fucked-up mood. The only thing that I could come up with was to keep it real with her and to tell her the truth. I just didn't want her to have to deal with more of my fucked-up ways. It was bad enough that I was knee-deep in the streets, and she already accepted all of the bad that came with me as it was. When I pulled up to the house, I saw that her car wasn't there. "Maybe it's in the garage," I thought to myself, and I headed inside.

Once I got into the house and saw that she wasn't home, I started to call her, but she didn't answer. I sent shorty a text, and she read my shit and didn't reply. She really had me fucked up. She'd been sitting around here, acting like a nigga had gone out and cheated and shit. But I knew one thing: when she brought her ass home, some shit was going to have to change. I was the king of this fucking house. I'm a good-ass nigga to my bitch. She just didn't understand that I lived two different lives. Shorty was really starting to piss me off with that attitude of hers. "I thought" she'd better fix that shit before shit went left. I had a little time to spare before she brought her ass home, so I decided to check out that nigga Meech. I prayed to God that nigga was who he said he was. "With all of the bullshit going on, the way Chyna's been acting, these sleepless nights, and no pussy, man—any nigga could get body bagged right now," I thought to myself as I headed out the front door.

Cinnamon

As I stood in front of the mirror to give myself the once-over, I had to give my man his props. But when he'd picked the dress out, he'd picked one that was a size too small—or I was gaining weight. Either way, I looked good, and the way the dress hugged my body and showed off all of my curves made it look even better on me. I loved the dress, but I planned on taking it off the moment I set eyes on my man. I wanted to make love to him in every way and in everyplace. I wanted to not only tell him how thankful I was but also to show him. After giving myself one last look, I grabbed my purse and the card I'd picked up on the way home—the one I'd put the ultrasound picture of our baby in. I headed out the door to meet my man. Not only was I looking like a million bucks, but I was also damn sure feeling like a million bucks. Couldn't nobody tell me shit.

I was feeling like Toni Braxton in that song "I Love Me Some Him," because for the first time in my life, I felt like I'd crossed roads with my soulmate. From the first time I'd set eyes on him, he'd made me feel a way no man had ever made me feel, and for the first time since we'd been together, I was no longer scared or afraid of all of the love I'd been trying to hide from him. I wanted to give him all of my love for the first time since I'd found out that I was about to become someone's mother. I was happy as hell to know that God had blessed us with a child, and I couldn't wait to tell him what I'd been keeping secret for the past week or so. I was in such a daze thinking about Malik and our baby that I never heard my phone go off. When I picked it up, I had three missed calls from Dominique. "That's strange," I thought to myself. He never called my phone. Before I could call him back, he was calling again.

"Hello," I said, answering the phone.

"Look, Cinnamon, I know that you ain't got shit to do with this, but tell your cousin that she's got one hour to bring her ass home before shit goes left. Shorty, I'm trying to give her a chance to get her fucked-up attitude together, but she's pushing me."

I was confused and didn't know what was going on. "As a matter of fact, I haven't talked to Chyna all week," I thought to myself.

"I don't know what's going on with y'all, but I haven't talked to Chyna all week. What did you do to my cousin?" I asked him.

"I haven't done shit to her yet. If you hear from her, tell her to bring her ass home."

"Yeah, ok," I said, and then I hung up. I would call Chyna tomorrow. Tonight was about my man and me. I just prayed that Dominique hadn't done anything out of line to Chyna. "I don't think he understands how crazy and smart Chyna is, but that's not for me to tell him," I said to myself as I pulled up to the Pin House.

I spotted Malik when I looked to my right. He was standing at the door with a suit on. I couldn't do anything but smile. No, this street-ass nigga wasn't in no suit. He looked good, standing at six foot two and with that fade that I loved so much and his chocolate skin tone. Every time I saw my man, he made my pussy throb and get wet. And that Italian suit from Ermenegildo that he was wearing made him look even better. I was happy to know that he could change it up from his street clothes to his grown-man look. I watched as he walked around the car to open my door and help me out.

"You look gorgeous," he said before giving me a kiss.

"Thank you, Zaddy. You look nice as well, and I loved everything you did for me today. Thank you."

"You're welcome, but I'm only doing what I promised you that I'd do from the start—and that is take care of you. But come on—we can talk about whatever you want when we get inside." Once we were inside, I began to smile from ear to ear. There were red rose petals everywhere, candles, and music. The more we walked, the more I could see how much work he'd put into this night. I couldn't stop smiling. I felt like a kid on Christmas who was about to open up a lot of gifts. Once we were at the table and seated, we just stared at each other for what seemed like a lifetime.

"Why do you always look at me like that?" I asked him.

"Why do you always ask me that question?" he asked me. "But to answer your question, sometimes when I look at you, I get lost in your beauty, and sometimes I sit and think about how lucky I am to have such a smart, hard-working woman. I'm not the best man out here, and I know I'm from the streets, but I'm no fool. I know what I have, and that's a queen. So when I look at you the way I do, it's not because I want a reaction out of you. It's because I'm actually lost when I look into your eyes. I feel like we were destined to be together and to cross roads."

I didn't know what to say. He had me speechless. All I could do was pull what he'd pulled on me.

"You know, you can go ahead and tell me that you're in love with me now." He smiled and did something that I hadn't been expecting him to do—he never broke eye contact with me when he said "I love you." I would be lying if I said that I didn't get butterflies when those words left his mouth. It wasn't because he told me that he loved me—it was because when he said it, I could feel it deep within myself, and it felt real and pure.

"I love you too, baby, and I'm so thankful that I have you as my man. Never in a million years would I have ever thought that I'd be in love with you or anyone else. You bring out the good in me and help balance me out. I love the fact that you can handle me in every way and that you don't let me run over you. But at the same time, you treat me like a queen. I'm blessed to have you, and I'm not afraid anymore to let you know that I'm in love with you, because I know we're meant to be."

"Now leave it up to him to say some off-the-wall shit," I thought.

"I knew you loved daddy," he said, winking at me.

I couldn't do anything but laugh. "You can never be serious," I said, still laughing.

"I was being serious, ma." When he said that, the in-house chef came to refill our wine glasses—or should I say *his* wine glass, because I hadn't touched mine. I wasn't sure what I could or couldn't have while I was pregnant, and I wasn't about to put my child in harm's way. Malik gave me a surprised look when I asked for water or juice. I didn't drink for the rest of the night. We ate and enjoyed each other's company until he stood up, walked around to my side of the table, and asked me to take his hand and to follow him. But as I grabbed his hand and stood up, he dropped down to one knee, and I swear that all of the air in my body left at that moment. I couldn't believe that he was really down on one knee with a big-ass ring. I didn't know if it was because of my hormones or because I was just happy, but I was crying hard like a kid who'd just gotten her ass beaten by her mama.

"Cinnamon, ever since the night you walked into my club, I knew that I had to have you. I could tell that you were different and something special. I never thought that you would make me fall in love and want more out of life than just the streets. When I'm with you, I can be myself. I don't have to try to impress you or buy you shit to keep you around. From day one, you showed me that it wasn't about my money. You see past all of the cars, money, clothes, and ice. I know I'm not perfect, and I still have some growing to do, but I wouldn't mind doing that growing with you. All I'm asking you to do is marry me and be my wife and continue to ride with me like you already have. I'm not saying that we have to get married right away, but, Cinnamon, will you be my wife?"

At that point I was crying uncontrollably. All I could do was shake my head up and down. Once he put the ring on my finger, I wrapped my arms around his neck and cried. I was so happy and speechless, and when I could finally get the words out, I said, "Hell, yes, I'll be your wife." For the rest of the night until the sun came up, we made love. If I hadn't already been pregnant, I would've been knocked up for damn sure after that night.

Chapter Seventeen

(Chyna) He's Insane

The last thing I remembered was that I'd been asleep in my hotel room, and then I woke up tied down to what seemed to be my bed. I tried to move, but I couldn't. My arms and legs were tied down. "How did I get here, and why the fuck am I tied down to my bed?" I thought to myself as I tried my best to move. But I couldn't move.

"You can try to move all you want, shorty, but you not going to be able to get loose."

"Dominique, what the fuck is going on, and why am I tied down to our bed?" He gave me a look that I'd never seen before—he just stood there staring at me like some fucking creep.

"Chyna, you know what type of nigga I am. Why'd you wanna go and play games, ma? Huh? You stayed gone all day and night then thought that I was going to just let you stay gone to the next day? What kind of nigga you take me for, shorty?" If I hadn't already known that this nigga was crazy before, then I knew it at that very moment. "You'd better be glad I didn't catch you with no nigga, or I would've made you help me chop that bitch-ass nigga up."

"Fuck you, Dominique. You think you can do whatever you want, but I can't? Nigga, you got me and life fucked up. You'd better be so glad I'm tied down to this bed, or I'd jump up and knock fire off yo' ass." He just looked at me as he rubbed his hands together.

"You know what, bae? You talk too fucking much," he said right before his head went between my legs. I hadn't even noticed that I didn't have any panties on. Fuck being tied down and held hostage. That nigga had a mouthpiece that would've put any bitch to sleep.

"Oh, oh shit, baby. Don't stop" was all I could get out. I couldn't run or kick or nothing—I had to lay there and let him suck the soul out of my pussy. Kevin Gates wasn't lying when he said, "Ever had lips on your booty and your pussy. Got your body feeling all mushy." The feeling he was giving me made my toes curl. I didn't know whether I was gonna cum because of what he was doing to my pussy or my ass, but I felt like I was getting ready to explode.

"Oh, baby, I'm about to cum. Oh—oh shit." As soon as those words left my mouth, he stopped, gave me a weird-ass smirk, and got up.

"Now lie there and think about the next time you call yourself wanting to pull one of those stunts," he said, and then he walked out of the room, leaving me hanging on the edge of an orgasm and tied down to the bed. I screamed his name over and over, but he never came back or answered me. As soon as that nigga untied me, it was going to be world war forty in this bitch.

Dominique

Chyna's ass thought she was slick, turning her phone off and staying gone all day. Shorty really didn't know what kind of nigga she was dealing with. I found her ass in less than thirty minutes. This little bitch who I used to fuck a while back told me that earlier that morning, Chyna had checked into the hotel she worked at. I gave shorty a few dollars, and she gave me a room key and her room number. When I got to her room, she was lying in bed asleep. I was happy to find out that she wasn't with no nigga. You can call it what you want, but I was in love with Chyna. She was the only woman I'd ever given my heart to. She understood me and didn't judge me, and she gave me peace of mind, which was something I'd rarely had. So body bagging a nigga over her wasn't shit to me. I didn't want my shorty out there trying to pay a nigga back because she thought I'd been out cheating on her, so I went and grabbed her. I gave her a little shot to keep her ass asleep till I got her back home.

Of course, she woke up talking shit, but I didn't care. I thought it was funny the way I ate her pussy and stop right before she was about to come. Chyna needed to learn who the king of this house was. I could hear her yelling and screaming my name all the way from the guest room, where I was washing my face and brushing my teeth. I had some business to take care of. You see, I hadn't been all of the way honest with Chyna about what I did for a living. I was a hit man who was paid to knock muthafuckas off. I never asked who'd placed the hit, because I didn't care. I got a kick out of body bagging muthafuckas. I only had one rule: no woman or children.

As I got dressed in all black to go grab this pasta-eating ass Italian's, I noticed that Chyna was a little too quiet. Once I was fully dressed, I looked inside our room and saw that she was sleep. I thought about untying her, but then I decided against it. I was gonna leave her ass just like that till I got back. I grabbed the keys to one of my run-down hoopties and left. It was Friday, and I knew that he loved to hang out at one particular strip club. It was my only chance to grab him—on every other day, he was always surround by a lot of security. When I pulled up to the club, I parked my car around back. I knew one of the strippers at the club and had paid her to leave the back door open for me.

Once I got into the club, I headed straight upstairs to the private VIP section for the ballers. I made sure to get a table diagonal from him so that he wouldn't notice me as I watched his every move. I grabbed a few strippers to dance for me. After watching him for about an hour, I waited until the same waitress who'd been bringing him drinks all night headed back to his table. When I saw that, I stood up and headed her way. When I walked past her, I bumped shorty a little—not hard enough to make her drop his drink but hard enough to distract her while I slipped something into it.

"My bad, ma. I'm a little fucked up," I said, slurring my words. Shorty just rolled her eyes and kept walking.

"Fuck her," I thought as I sat at the bar and ordered a shot of Hennessy. I waited for about ten minutes and then looked over my left shoulder to catch a glimpse of him. Any minute, he'd have to run to the bathroom, and right on cue, he began to throw up as he tried to push one of the strippers off of his lap. I waited for a minute and then walked to the bathroom he was in. He had one man guarding the door and another man with him. As I walked closer to the bathroom, I began to walk like I was drunk, and the man put his hand up to me and told me to use the bathroom on the other side of the room. I started to lean and stumble like I was going to fall on him. I reached into my waistband and grabbed the Glock with the silencers on it—he never saw it coming. I gave him two to the chest and pushed him through the door. The man on the other side of the door didn't have time to reach for his gun. I gave him a clean shot to the head and then kicked open the door of the stall that my target was in. He was leaning over the toilet still throwing up.

"Aye," I said, and right when he looked back, I gave him two to the head and one to the heart. I stood over him and reached into my back pocket to grab my razor. I put some gloves on and reached down to cut his lips off. "Loose lips sink ships, bitch." I threw his lips into a plastic bag and put them in my pocket. On the way out of the bathroom, I gave the man I'd shot in the chest two to the head as well. I had to make sure that everyone was dead. I threw my hood over my head, hit the lights, and walked out, making sure that no one saw me go.

Once I was outside, I jumped in my car and left. I drove for about forty-five minutes until I came to the junkyard I owned under a false name. After pulling up to it, I got out and walked over to my Benz to grab a duffel bag of clothes. I changed, threw the clothes I'd taken off into the car, and crushed it over and over again. I used the machine to pick up the car and moved it to the other side of the yard so that it could be melted down. Once everything was done, I jumped in my Benz and headed home to Chyna. The last thing I wanted was for her to wake up still tied down and without me there again. All I wanted to do was go home to my bitch and get in her guts.

"Big Malik, a.k.a. the "Grim Reaper"
I sat outside of my ex-wife's house, watching her from a distance. She was still as fine as she had been the day I'd met her. Yvette had always been a go-getter bitch—that was what had made me fall for her in the first place, but her beauty was a plus. I'd never thought I'd see the day when we would part ways. We'd been the black Bonnie and Clyde—or so I'd thought. I would never understand why she'd done me the way she had. Our daughter had just turned one when I went away. The fact that I was missing out on seeing my kids grow up used to fuck with me all of the time, but the older they got, the more I wondered why they never came to visit me, wrote me, or reached out to me. My heart was broken. My only family members had turned their backs on me when I'd needed them the most. And the sad part about it was that I still loved my ex-wife, but I knew that shit was dead wood. It had been "fuck me" for the last twenty years, but now it was "fuck them." The streets of Chicago is mine. The Grim Reaper was back, and I'd kill anything and everything that stood in my way. After watching her for another twenty minutes, I drove off. It was time to let the streets know that the original king was back. It'd be like I'd never left.

Chapter Eighteen

(Cinnamon)
Nothing Lasts Forever

My night was short-lived as I lay on the bathroom floor, holding my stomach. This baby was taking the life right out of me. What happened to all of the stories about how beautiful pregnancy is and all of that bullshit? Ever since I'd found out that I was pregnant, all I'd been doing every morning was throw up, but all through the day, I would be fine—just tired and sleepy. I couldn't wait to go to my first doctor's appointment. I wanted to know what I could do about the morning sickness. I heard Malik moving around in the other room. I'd yet to tell him about the baby. I'd been planning on telling him the night before, but after he gave me that big-ass ring, all we did was make love everywhere until I feel asleep in his arms. I felt like the luckiest woman alive, and couldn't nobody take that away from me. I sat up straight on the bathroom floor. I needed to shower and brush my teeth. Right when I was about to get off of the floor, Malik walked into the bathroom with a confused look on his face.

"Why are you on the floor?" he asked while helping me up. I tried to cover my mouth while I talked to him because I'd been throwing up all morning and hadn't brushed my teeth yet.

"Bae, I wasn't feeling good, so I came in here just in case I had to throw up," I said while turning toward the sink and grabbing a toothbrush.

He stood there staring at me for the longest time with a weird look on his face. It was like he was trying to read my body or me, but I didn't pay him no attention and instead continued to brush my teeth.

"So when are you planning on telling me that you're pregnant with my seed?" When he said that, I spit out the water that I'd been rinsing my mouth out with.

The first thought that crossed my mind was "How did he know?" And the look on his face told me that he knew for sure that I was pregnant.

"I'm not stupid, Cinnamon. I pay attention to your body. Your titties are getting bigger, you're sleeping too much, you didn't drink or smoke last night, and now you're sick. Plus, I can feel that you're carrying my seed. Why are you hiding it, shorty? Don't tell me that you were thinking about getting rid of it." When he said that, I got really pissed off because I didn't believe in abortions.
"Damn, you really think that little of me? You think I'd kill our baby?" I asked him.

"I didn't say that. I'm just trying to figure out why you felt the need to hide it from me—that's all." At that point he had me hot and pissed off. I didn't want to talk to that nigga about shit. Instead I walked out of the bathroom with him right on my heels. I walked over to my purse to get the card I'd bought him—the one with the ultrasound picture of our baby in it. I handed it to him.

"Here. I was planning to give this to you last night, but since you think you know it all, you can sit here and open it up by yourself," I said while walking back to the bathroom. I started the shower. I couldn't believe he'd thought that I'd kill our baby. I mean, don't get me wrong—I hadn't been too happy when I'd found out, but I never could've killed something that was a part of me.

I really wanted to watch him open the card. I loved what it said on the outside. It read, "I'm glad God chose you to walk through this thing called life with me. I know you have been a good man, but you'll be an even better man to me." Then there was an arrow, and the inside of the card said, "I can't wait to meet you, Daddy," and the ultrasound picture was in it. But he'd just had to fuck it up with his big-ass mouth.

"He thinks he knows everything, so he can sit and read it by himself," I thought to myself as I stood under the shower and let the water run down my body. For some odd reason, whenever I got in the shower, my whole body would relax. My titties wouldn't hurt, and the sickness would go away. As I stood there just letting the warm water hit my body, I felt Malik wrap his arms around my waist. I knew my man's touch. I could've been in a house full of people, and I still wouldn't have had to turn around to see who it was. I knew his touch, and so did my body.

He pulled me closer to him and whispered, "I'm sorry, baby." I didn't pay that shit any mind—he needed to be sorry for saying the bullshit he'd said. I just wanted to take a shower in peace. He'd fucked my morning up with that comment he'd made. I went to reach for a towel so that I could wash my face, but he stopped me and turned me around to face him. I can't lie—just looking at my man with his rock-hard dick hanging like a horse's turned me on and made my pussy start to throb and get wet.

"I said I'm sorry, baby. I didn't mean to put you in a bad mood. The last thing I want to do is put the mother of my child in a fucked-up mood. While you're carrying my seed, all I want to do is take care of you and my seed. Ma, can you just forgive a nigga?"

As I stood there and listened to everything he said, I couldn't help but forgive him. I'd never heard this man apologize for shit he'd done or said. Usually it was either his way or his way, so hearing him say sorry meant a lot, especially because he was a person who never used that word at all.

"I forgive you, Zaddy. Just don't let no shit like that come out of your mouth again, or we're going to have some problems." Instead of immediately replying, he backed me up against the shower wall and kissed me.

"I love you" was all he said before he knelt down and put one of my legs on his shoulder.

He started to eat my pussy like it was the last supper. I held his head in place and moved my hips back and forth as I moaned. "I love you too," I said. For the rest of the afternoon, we made love in the shower, on the counter tops in the kitchen, and in the Jacuzzi. I was getting dressed to go out and spend the rest of the day with my man when I heard him breaking shit and yelling at somebody on the phone. Moments later he burst into the bathroom with a look in his eyes that I'd never seen before and never wanted to see again.

"Grab all of your shit. We have to go now!" he yelled before walking out of the bathroom. I tried to ask him what was going on, but he just snapped at me. "I said, get your shit. Or leave it—I don't give a fuck. But we have to go now. I'll explain everything later."

Malik

Waking up that morning and then finding out that Cinnamon was carrying my seed had a nigga feeling different. I felt a joy that I'd never felt before in my life. I was about to be someone's father. I'd always told myself that when I had kids, I wouldn't be like my father, a bitch-ass nigga who'd left my mother with three kids to take care of by herself. My son or daughter would know who his or her father was and wouldn't have to question my love. I would've painted the world red behind my seed, and he or she wasn't even in the world yet.

I was happy to know that I had a solid-ass relationship with my girl. I'd known when I'd first met Cinnamon that she was going to be the mother of my kids. But little did she know that a nigga wanted an army full of kids. The moment she dropped the one she was carrying, I was going to put another one in her. I figured that she might as well get ready to quit her job. The only job she was going to have was the one where she married me and took care of the house and our kids. What would I look like if let the mother of my child work even though her man was a multimillionaire? She had to get that out of her head right away.

I had just gotten dressed and was waiting for Cinnamon. I'd asked her what she wanted to do today, and she'd said that she wanted to eat and spend the day with me. That was why I loved her and had nothing but the utmost respect for her. She didn't ask for much—just for simple things. I was smoking a blunt and watching the news. Somebody had knocked off this big-time Italian drug lord and had left him lipless in a strip club's bathroom. Then Markese called me saying that our truck with all of the money and product in it had been hit, and all three of my traps houses had been burned to the ground. A nigga got sick when he heard that shit.

"What the fuck you mean, my traps got burned down, and my truck got hit?" I wasn't trying to hear the shit this nigga was saying. All I saw was red. I ran these muthafucking streets. A muthafucka wouldn't dare to even think twice about crossing me, and knowing that somebody had the balls to do it had me beyond pissed. I wasn't in the mood to keep talking to that nigga. "Call everybody, and meet me at my house in twenty minutes," I said before hanging up on him and throwing the phone, breaking it into pieces. I was so in shock that I began to break up everything that I could reach out and touch. I couldn't think straight. I took off and ran upstairs to tell Cinnamon that we had to go. I felt kind of bad for yelling at my shorty, but fuck all that shit. I didn't have time to worry about her feelings—I'd explain everything to her later. Once we were in the car, I drove at one hundred miles per hour on the interstate, praying the whole way there that I didn't get pulled over and end up in jail. I wasn't going to stop until I got home. Once I pulled up, I saw Markese, and Dominique was there with Chyna.

Before I could park the car, Cinnamon got out, slammed the door, and stomped into the house. I wasn't up for her shit. There was about to be a war in the streets, and the last thing I needed was a war going on at my home front too. I looked over at Markese and Dominique as I walked toward the front door. "Where the fuck are Zilla and Choppa?" I asked.

"They should be pulling up any minute now," Markese said. Once I was in the house, I ran upstairs to change. I threw on an all-black sweat suit and some all-black Timberlands. After I was dressed, I went back downstairs to my office and walked past Cinnamon and Chyna. If looks could've killed, I would've been in a body bag, the way my girl was looking at me. Once I was in my office, I poured a shot of Hennessy and sparked up a blunt.

All I could think was "Who could've done this, and why?" By the time Dominique, Markese, Zilla, and Choppa came into my office, I was on my fifth shot of Hennessy, and I wasn't in the mood to play around with a soul about my money or my drugs. When I looked up at Choppa, I saw that he had two choppers with him: one in his hand and one hanging off of his shoulder. I could see that everybody's face looked like mine—puzzled and confused. "I'ma make this quick, because the longer we sit here, the shittier I'm going to get. I want anybody and everybody who had something to do with this in a body bag within an hour. I don't give a fuck about how many people we have to kill. We'll keep going until we find out who did this. Our first stop is that nigga Meech. Shit didn't start happening until that nigga came into town. Dominique, you got eyes on him?"

"Yeah, I know where he's at. I bugged his car. I can tell you his every move within the last twenty-four hours."

"Good, let's go grab that nigga. We're not gonna stop until the niggas who took from us are dead." Right when I said that, as if on cue, everybody in the room cocked their shit. I grabbed my .45 caliber and tucked it into my waistband. Then I opened up the wall behind my desk, exposing choppers, big-ass machine guns, and bombs that would've taken out a whole building.

"Oh shit," Choppa said. "Let me get that chopper right there. That muthafuck is sick," he said, picking it up.

"Nigga, what you gonna do with three big-ass Choppers?" Zilla asked.

"Shit, you'll see. When it's time to lay these pussy-ass niggas down, you'll be happy that a nigga brought all three," he said as he held the chopper in the air and looked at it. I grabbed a chopper, and so did Markese and Zilla. Dominique never used choppers—he said he didn't need them. He gave niggas head shots. On the way out the door, I looked over at Cinnamon, who looked pissed.

"Damn, a nigga can't win for losing," I thought to myself as I walked out the front door. We jumped into my Benz and left. We were gonna grab that nigga Meech and whoever he had with him.

Yvette

It had been a long time since I'd hit a blunt. I'd given that life up a long time ago, when my ex-husband had gone to prison. You see, I had a past of my own that I wasn't too proud of. I was always the woman with the plan, and my husband was the man with the vision. I'd been a hustler way before I'd met my ex-husband. I was the one who'd put him on and brought him into the game. I'd never cared too much about the street life. When my mother passed away, my grandmother took in my two sisters and me and raised all three of us. Long story short my grandfather was a trained hit man, and my grandmother was a big-time drug dealer. I'd always wondered why my mother had never wanted us around our grandparents, and I then found out why.

When she passed away, my grandmother and grandfather raised us to be some hustlers. They turned us into savages at a young age by showing us the ins and outs of the drug game. My older sister never cared about the drug game—she was more interested in what my grandfather did for a living, and she went on to become one of the best hit women who's still living to this day. My sisters and I had been born and raised in Detroit. Then when I came on a business run to Chicago, I met Malik and fell in love. What my ex-husband failed to realize, though, was that I'd always been TTG and that I would always outsmart him.

I knew that Malik—or should I say "the Grim Reaper"—was out of jail. For the last three months, I'd been sitting and waiting for him to make his move. I was no fool—I knew deep inside of me that Big Malik would be out for revenge. But he'd fucked up when he'd gone after my kids. He was still pissed that I'd left him in prison to rot. I'd told him from the jump that after we had Malik Jr., I wanted out of the street life so that I could raise my son the right way—and, needless to say, I said that if he ended up getting time, I wouldn't stay with him. But I let him talk me into staying with him.

After I had Markese, I began to put money away. I knew that I was going to leave him, but then I ended up pregnant with Mariah. Not even a year after she was born, he caught a case down in Miami. I took that chance to get my kids and myself far away from him. Malik had never cared about our kids the way I did. His only concerns were the streets and becoming the biggest kingpin to ever live. He had no respect for anyone, and he didn't care who he had to cross to get to the top.

I had told my kids some lies, and I had to be woman enough to fix that. I never wanted my kids to grow up to live the life their father and I had lived. I'd tried my best to keep my son Malik out of the streets, but it seemed like the lies I'd told him had only led him to the streets anyway. I would have never told my son this, but I was proud of him. He'd done what his father never could've done without my help, and that was take over the streets of Chicago. My son had been born a king, and he'd worked hard to get where he was. Big Malik thought he'd won by burning down my son's trap house and taking his shipment, but what my ex-husband failed to realize was that I was the original trap queen.

Before I'd let my son lose everything he'd worked so hard for, I'd step back into that kitchen, and it would be like I'd never left. My name alone carried weight, so when I placed a call to my old Coloumbian connect, it was nothing for him to ship me out a few kilos of the purest cocaine to hit the streets of Chicago since the late '70s or early '80s. I'd be damned if I let a tender-dick nigga try to break my son. I had a plan that would work, but first I had to find my son. He was a lot like his father—he had a dark side to him, and I knew that he'd already be out tearing up the streets of Chicago. I had to find him and tell him everything I knew.

They always say that what's done in the dark in time will come to the light. The last thing I wanted was for my son and I to fall out because of my lies. Malik was my pride and joy. He reminded me of myself, and I didn't want to lose my son because of this. I continued to hit my blunt as I drove to the airport to pick up my big sister. It had been years since we'd last seen each other, but every month she would send me a post card to let me know that she was fine. The last time I'd seen her had been at our sister's funeral. We didn't see much of each other or talk much due to the fact that she was a big-time hit woman, but my son and I needed her. She'd always told me that no matter what, she'd always have my back, and she'd given me a number to use only in case of an emergency. This was an emergency, and I needed her because one, I didn't know anybody else alive who could move like she could, and two, together we could make some of the best crack, and my son needed it and both of us.

For about twenty minutes, I sat and waited for her to walk out of the airport. I'd told her what kind of car I would be in, but I still didn't see no sign of her. I waited for about another ten minutes, and then I heard my car door open, and she got in. She wasted no time and told me to drive the moment she got into the car. Just seeing my sister in the flesh made me want to cry. To be laying eyes on her meant the world to me. She was still in good shape and very beautiful, like our mother had been.

"I had to make sure you weren't being followed. That's what took me so long," she said.

"I figured you were around here somewhere. Thank you so much for coming on short notice. You know I wouldn't have called if I didn't truly need you."

"You don't have to thank me. You're my sister, and any problem that you have is my problem. But I will say this: we wouldn't be having this problem if you'd let me knock that nigga off when he was in jail. Now look at the bullshit he's on. I've told you since day one that he's a snake and that something about him isn't right. Now here he is, coming after his own blood."

"I know, Porsha. But he is the father of my kids—I didn't want him dead."

"Fuck all that shit. That nigga don't give a fuck about y'all. I mean, look at the shit he's doing. I didn't come all this way to play games. If my nephew doesn't plan on body bagging that nigga, then I'm damn sure gonna do it. Have you at least told them the truth about everything yet?"

"No, I haven't. I planned on doing that after I got you."

She let out a deep breath and shook her head. "I told you out of the gate to tell those kids the truth. Why you think we was so fucked up when Grandma and Papa finally got to see us? Because Mama was keeping secrets from us. I understand why you did it, but he still ended up doing everything that you didn't want him to do. I hear everything that goes on. I keep eyes on my family at all times. If grandma were alive, she'd be proud of Malik. He's a lot like her, and he runs a pretty good operation to the point that the pigs can't pin shit on him.

"And speaking of that, we have an even bigger problem. Dominique reached out to me for some info on a man named Meech—he couldn't find anything on him. Well, I dug a little deeper," she said, pulling out a folder with some papers in it. As I came to a red light, I opened the folder, and my mouth dropped when I read everything that was inside of it. I was in such a daze that I didn't see the light turn green, and the drivers behind me began to blow their horns.

"I need to find my son right now," I said to my sister as I handed her the folder.

"I know, but do me a favor, and let me tell him about this. I'm sure that after he finds out the truth about everything, he's not going to want to hear shit else that you have to say, and this will only make matters worse. But in the meantime, I want you to drop me off at this hotel."

"Ok, but why are you going to a hotel? I have plenty of room at my house."

"It's not about that. I have some business to handle. I'll meet back up with you in two hours, max."

After dropping Porsha off, I headed back home. I couldn't believe that my life was getting ready to take a turn for the worse—and not only my life but also my son's. What I'd read in that file had made my mind race. I had no choice but to stick it out with my son. He was gonna need all of the help he could get, because shit was about to hit the fan—hard.

Chapter Nineteen

(Malik)
Only Time Will Tell

"I'ma ask you this one time and one time only: Where the fuck is my money and my shipment, and who the fuck sent you?" I asked Meech. He and two of his boys were ass naked and tied down to a table. All of my patience had gone out the window the moment my traps had been burned down, and my shipment had been hit. So I wasn't trying to hear shit but who'd burned down my shit and who'd taken my product and money.

"I swear to God, Malik—I swear on my kids, man. I don't know what you're talking about."

"Wrong fucking answer," I said, getting up and walking over to a table full of shit that would get that muthafucka talking. As I put on an apron, I could hear Meech still talking and pleading with me and asking me to believe him. I didn't believe shit that he said, because shit hadn't started happening until that nigga had brought his ass into town. After I had my apron on, I looked through the knives on the table and came across a big-ass, sharp machete. The whole time I was looking at the blade of the machete, I was walking over to one of his homeboys. I wasn't up for playing games, and I didn't like to repeat myself or feel like I was being bullshitted.

174

Once I was close enough to him, I wasted no time. I raised the machete and then brought it down as hard as I could onto one of his hands. To my surprise, after the first swing, his whole hand fell off and hit the ground. I'd thought that I was going to have to hit it three or four times before the whole hand would fall off. The screams from the nigga whose hand I'd just cut off were so loud that everybody but a dead body would've heard him if I hadn't had soundproof walls.

"You see, Meech, every time I ask you a question and you give me bullshit, I'ma make you watch me cut your boys up until I eventually get to you." I looked over at the dude whose hand I'd just cut off. He was looking like he wanted to pass out. "Fuck all that," I thought to myself.

"Aye, Dominique. Give that nigga a shot, and wake his ass back up. We're just getting started. And stop the bleeding before that nigga bleeds out and dies. I'm not done with him just yet."

"I was wondering when you were going to ask," he said while walking toward me and handing me a blunt. I looked over at Markese. He was smoking a blunt without a care in the world. He was used to this shit, but Zilla and Choppa, on the other hand, looked like they were trying their best to keep straight faces. Shooting and torturing a muthafucka are two different things. I walked back over to where Meech was and pulled a chair up next to him. I hit the blunt a few times and blew the smoke in his face.

"I'm good at reading people, and something tells me that he's telling the truth. But like I said before, shit didn't start happening until he came into town, so right now, unless I know for sure that he didn't do it, he and his niggas will be floating with the fishes by tonight."

I snapped out of my thoughts when I heard screaming. I looked over, and Dominique was burning the nigga's wound to stop the bleeding. I looked back down at Meech, who looked like he was ready to shit himself.

"Now we can do this all day if you want. I have enough drugs here to keep you muthafuckas alive long enough for me to continue torturing y'all. The choice is yours," I said. Before he could respond, the other nigga who was tied down began to talk shit from across the room.

"Fuck these pussy-ass niggas, Meech. These bitch-ass niggas are going to kill us whether we did it or not."

After he said that, Markese, Zilla, and Choppa got up and beat the shit out of him. I watched and let it go on for a few minutes, and then I stopped them. I finished smoking my blunt before I walked over to him. He looked up at me with swollen eyes and blood running out of his mouth. What he did next shocked me. He cocked his head back and spit on me. I looked down at the spit on my apron and laughed.

"You know what, young'un? You got heart—a lot of heart—and big balls, you could even say. You know, if shit wasn't going down like this, I probably would've put you on my team." The whole time I was talking to him, I was looking through the knives to find the sharpest one. Once I found the one I liked, I put some gloves on and turned back around to him. "So you got big balls, huh?"

"Fuck you, bitch-ass nigga."

"This nigga doesn't know when to shut up," I thought as I smirked about what he'd said. "No, fuck you," I said, and I cut his balls off. I began to laugh at his cries and screams. "What you crying for?" I asked between laughs. "You got big balls, remember? Take that shit like a man, pussy." I looked over at Markese. He was shaking his head. "Nigga, come hold his mouth open," I said to Markese. And moments later he was up and putting gloves on. Once his mouth was open, I took his balls and forced them into his mouth, causing him to throw up. I looked up when I heard somebody else throwing up. It was Zilla. I wasn't surprised. I remembered the first time I'd seen someone get done like this—it'd fucked me up too.

I looked over to the table and saw a blowtorch. "Aye, Dominique, hand me that blowtorch, fam."

Markese looked at me like, "What you about to do with that?" Once I had the blowtorch, I went ahead and burned the rest of that nigga's dick off. The smell of his burning flesh almost made me want to throw up. That nigga was a bitch and a pussy, so I gave him one. There was no point in giving him a shot to keep him alive—that nigga had been dead the moment I'd put his balls in his mouth.

"Maybe next time, he'll learn to keep his mouth shut," I thought to myself as I walked over to Markese, who was taking shots of Hennessy back to back. I asked him to pour me a shot. My mind wouldn't stop racing, and I wasn't going to rest until I found out who'd hit my shipment and burned down my traps. I looked back to Zilla, who was sitting down, holding his stomach, and shaking his head. "He'll be all right," I thought to myself. Right when I was getting ready to walk back over to Meech, my phone began to go off. I looked at my phone and saw that it was my mama. I didn't have time to talk to her, but she wouldn't stop calling, so I went ahead and answered it.

"Aye, Ma, I'ma have to call you back—" But before I could get the rest out, she began to talk, and what she was saying was enough to keep me on the phone. "I'm on my way," I told her, and then I hung up. "Come on, y'all. We have to go. We'll finish these niggas off when we come back."

"What? Where are we going? We just gonna leave them here like that?" Markese asked.

"That was Mama. She said that she knows for a fact who hit our shipment and burned down the traps. Fuck these niggas. One of them's dead, and the other two ain't going nowhere. We'll finish them off later." When I said that, everybody jumped up and headed for the door.

Cinnamon

I guess it's true when they say that nothing good lasts for long. How did I go from waking up and making love to my soon-to-be husband to rushing out of the Pin House and then to this bullshit? I knew the type of life Malik lived and the kind of man I was dealing with, but it seemed like he didn't know what kind of woman he had. I'm not one to bitch or complain, but I feel like no matter what's going on in the streets, you're never supposed to leave your home unhappy. I knew about everything that was going on, and the last thing I wanted to do was add fuel to the fire. I wanted to be my man's peace, not his headache. I thought that as his woman, I was supposed to hold him down at home and when it came to the streets.

At this point I really wished that I could smoke a blunt to calm my nerves. I didn't know if it was because I was truly in love with Malik or if my hormones were making me feel that way, but I couldn't stop praying in my head that everything would be ok with him. I'd never been so worried in my life. This was the last thing I wanted to happen between us. I told myself that after that day, I wouldn't ever let him leave the house on bad terms. Knowing that there was a chance that he wouldn't come home, I said one last prayer to God, asking him to watch over not only Malik but also Markese, Choppa, Dominique, and Zilla. I snapped out of my thoughts when I heard Chyna walk back into the living room.

"Girl, you still over there pissed off because Malik yelled at you? When did you become so damn sensitive?" she asked me.

"But what if something happened to him?" I thought to myself. I'd let him walk out of the house without making things right.

"Fuck you, Chyna," I said. "I'm not mad at the fact that he yelled at me. I'm pissed off because he could've handled the situation better."

"Well, at least you only got yelled at. Hell, be happy that you wasn't kidnapped and tied down to a bed for hours."

I had to let what she'd said register in my head. "What are you talking about, Chyna?"

"Girl, Dominique's ass came and found me at the hotel I was staying in and drugged me up. When I woke up, I was at home and tied down to our bed with no panties on."

I couldn't do anything but laugh, because who would do something like that? "Why were you at a hotel in the first place?" I asked her in between laughs.

"It's not funny, Cinnamon. He really did kidnap me, and he held me hostage. He thought he could bring his ass into the house at seven in the morning one day. I didn't argue with him, and I didn't mention shit about it. I let him think that shit was all good, because two can play that game. So I stayed gone all day and night like he'd done. He had me fucked up if he thought that I was going to let that shit slide."

"Well, it looks like you lost that game," I said, and we both began to laugh. Then my phone began to ring, and it was Mariah. She said that she was pulling up. "Good, because I'm hungry," I said to her. She'd called me right after Malik had left to ask if I had any plans. I said that with everything that had happened, I needed a girls' day to take my mind off of all of the bullshit that was going on. But what I really wanted was for my man to come home and for everything to go back to how it had been when we'd woken up that morning. I put my phone down and went to open the door for Mariah. When I got to the door, she was finishing up a blunt that she'd just rolled.

"What's up, sis," she asked while walking into the house.

"Not much, girl. Come on. Chyna and I are sitting in the living room talking," I said as I walked back to the living room.

"What's up, Chyna?" Mariah asked as she passed her the blunt.

"Girl, same shit, different day. Just dealing with your crazy-ass brother."

Mariah began to laugh. "Join the club. I've been dealing with all three of them my whole life." Mariah paused. "Oh my God," she said as she reached for my left hand.

"Leave it up to Mariah to spot the ring on my finger," I thought.

"Bitch, when did this happen?" she asked.

"When did what happen?" Chyna asked, looking all lost in the face until she looked down at my hand. "Oh shit, bitch," she said, jumping up to get a closer look at my ring. "I've been here all this time and didn't even notice. Damn, that's a nice-ass ring. Congratulations—I can't wait to be in the wedding."

"Me too," Mariah said. "Congratulations, sis. Now you'll officially be my sister. I can't believe my brother is about to get married. My mama is going to take over everything—you know that, right?"

"Thanks, y'all. And that's what Malik said too. Y'all should have seen me and how I was crying when he asked me to marry him last night. He had me crying like I'd just gotten my ass beaten by my mama or something. I'm so happy—I can't wait to start planning the wedding," I said as Chyna tried to pass me the blunt. I shook my head no, and she looked at me like I'd just turned down a million dollars.

"Since when don't you smoke?" Chyna asked. Everything had been happing so fast that I hadn't had a chance to tell anyone about the engagement or the baby.

"I'm pregnant—" I started to say, and both Chyna and Mariah began to yell with excitement.

"What else have you been keeping from us?" Mariah said.

"That's what I'm saying. I don't talk to you for a week, and here it comes out that you're about to get married and have my baby cousin. I'm hoping it's a girl."

"Me too," Mariah said. "I'm the last and only girl in my family. We need girls. I'm about to be an auntie—I can't wait!"

All I could do was smile. It seemed like everything was all good, and everybody was happy for Malik and me. Just thinking about our baby made me realize that I had everything I'd ever wanted.

"I know Malik wants a boy, but I'm with Chyna. I'm hoping for a little girl."

"Yeah, I'm hoping for a girl too. We had planned to tell everybody today, but then all of this bullshit happened. It really fucked up the day we had planned."

"Yeah, my mama told me what happened. I know my brothers are probably out tearing up the streets as we speak. I just pray for whoever it was that crossed my brother—that's the last thing he should have ever done," Mariah said. I let what she'd said to me sink in.

"I'm praying like hell that my man makes it back home in one piece," I said. For the next hour, we sat and talked, and then we decided to go eat and see a movie. We were halfway to the restaurant when Mama Yvette called. She told Mariah to get home because she had to talk to her about something important. We didn't mind riding with her, since we were already in the car. On the way to her house, I had Mariah stop and get me some food. I was feeling sick because I was so hungry and hadn't eaten since earlier. Once we pulled up to Mama Yvette's house, we got out of the car, and Malik, Zilla, Dominique, Choppa, and Markese got out of another car.

Unexpected Crossroads
(Yvette)

As I sat in my living room smoking a blunt and taking shots of Hennessy, I looked through my kids' baby pictures. I felt like I'd failed as a mother and filled their heads with lies. I hadn't done it to hurt them—I'd done it to save them from the kind of life that their father, their grandparents, and I had lived. I did to them what my mother had done to her kids. The longer I sat, the more nervous I became. My kids would be arriving at any minute, and I had to tell them that everything I'd ever told them while they were growing up had been a lie. I was just hoping and praying that they'd forgive me and understand that I'd done what any mother would've done at the time. I never wanted to lie or mislead my kids, but I couldn't take back what I'd done—and even if I could've, I wouldn't have. At the time, that had been the best choice for all of us, and I had to live with that.

As I continued to smoke my blunt, I heard my front door open, and voices filled my house. I took a deep breath and said a quick prayer. I heard my son Malik call my name as they walked through the house, looking for me. "I'm in here," I yelled out from the living room. When he walked in and saw me smoking a blunt, he had a clueless look on his face, and everyone else looked clueless too.

"Ma, what are you doing smoking?" Malik asked me.

I took a deep breath and hit the blunt before I spoke. "Everyone, come in, and sit down, please. I have something to tell you." Everyone was confused, and everyone was there, even Cinnamon and Chyna. I didn't feel that I needed to hold anything back in front of them, because in my eyes, since my sons had brought them home, they were family as well. I poured a shot of Hennessy before I stood up. After I took the shot, I took a good look around my living room, and my heart became warm.

"This is my family, and I don't want to lose them," I thought to myself.

"Ma, what's going on? Why'd you call us all here?" Markese asked me.

I looked over at my oldest, Malik, and I could tell that he was becoming inpatient. "First off, I want to say to my kids that I love you all very much, and I want you all to let me finish what I have to say before you judge me. Before you all were born, your father and I were some big-time drug dealers. I learned the game from your great-grandparents at a young age. When my mother passed away, my grandparents took my sisters, and me in and taught us the ins and outs of the drug game. My grandfather was one of the best hit men to ever live, and my grandmother was one of the biggest queenpins out of Detroit.

"When I took a business trip to Chicago, I met your father and fell in love. I eventually moved to Chicago to help your father take over the streets. I put your father on and showed him what my grandmother had showed me, but when I got pregnant with you, Malik, I wanted out. I wanted to raise my kids and to be a full-time mother, not one who was cooking crack over the stove. But your father convinced me to stay with him anyway, and I ended up pregnant with you, Markese. When that happened, I began to stash money to get away because I knew that I wanted better for my kids, and all your father wanted was to make a name for himself. And his name is one that many still know to this day—the Grim Reaper."

As I continued to talk, my kids had looks of disbelief on their faces— they couldn't believe what I was telling them. "After having you, Markese, two years later, I had Mariah. Your father ended up going to Miami on one of his normal runs, and the feds picked him up. When word got back to me, I took that as a sign that I should leave. I left him to rot in prison for the last twenty years."

"Hold the fuck up. You're meaning to tell me that my father has been in prison this whole time, and you let us believe that he just walked out of our lives?" Malik said. At that point he was standing up, and the look on his face could have killed.

"Yes, he's been in prison. I know that you're mad, but what you will not do is disrespect me in my house. I'm still you mother, and don't you forget that. I did what was best for my kids at the time. Your father was bringing our family down, and if I hadn't taken y'all and left, then I would've lost y'all as well. Don't sit here and judge me for a muthafucking thing. Yes, I'm sorry that I lied to keep you safe. I didn't want any of my kids to live the life that your father and I lived. I will not apologize for wanting better for my kids and for keeping them safe."

"So lying to us is keeping us safe?" he asked me. At that point I walked up to my son because he must've forgotten who the fuck I was.

Once I was close enough to his face, I looked him dead in the eye. "You have one more time to disrespect me, and then I'ma show you that you forgot just who the fuck I am. Now sit the fuck down, and let me finish what I have to say. If you want to leave after that, you can, but you will sit and listen to what I have to say."

For a minute we just stood there looking at each other. You would have thought that it was just us in the room. Once he sat back down, I continued to talk. "Now, your father was sentenced to twenty-five to life, but he's been out for the last three months. He doesn't know that I know that he's out. I've always been ten steps ahead of your father. I know him inside and out, and I know for a fact that he was the one who burned down your traps and took your shipment. He's out for revenge for what I did, and the only way to hurt me is by hurting you."

"What the fuck?" Markese said as he stood up. "You're meaning to tell me that our father is the one behind all of this? Why would he want to take his kids out?"

"To get back at me, I'm guessing." I looked up at my son Malik, and my heart began to hurt. The look in his eyes made it clear that he was disgusted with me. I wanted to cry because I'd never wanted to hurt my son, and I had. Everyone in the room looked speechless.

"You know what, Ma?" Malik said as he stood up. "I always hated my father because I felt like he walked out on us. I always told myself that if I ever came across him, I would body bag him because he'd left you high and dry. But you're the one I hate. You didn't have to lie to me. I can't believe this shit."

"Well, son, you can hate me till the end of time, but I'm still your mother, and can't nothing change that." Just as I was saying that, the doorbell began to ring, and nobody made a move. For the first time since I'd started talking, I noticed my daughter, Mariah, whose face looked like everyone else's. She didn't say anything but instead got up to open the door. When she didn't say who it was or come back fast enough, I got a feeling in my stomach that something wasn't right. I reached under the couch and grabbed my .45. My sons must've felt the same way, because they pulled out their guns as well.

Right as I was getting ready to walk to the front door, my ex-husband came walking into the living room with his gun pressed against Mariah's back. My heart dropped when I saw that. He still looked the same—he was tall, dark, and handsome, and he looked just like my son Malik.

"Put your guns down. I'm not going to hurt my daughter," he said while tucking his gun into his waistband and letting Mariah go. "Long time, no see," he said, never breaking eye contact with me. I didn't put my gun away. I didn't trust that nigga as far I could throw him. "Come on now, Yvette. Put the gun down. There's a houseful of people, and I'm sure they're not going to let me hurt you. You are my wife, remember?"

I smirked because that nigga loved playing games. "Now, you and I both know that I haven't been your wife for twenty years. And as for me putting this gun down—well, it'll be a cold day in hell before I put it down."

He smiled a little and then looked over at Malik. "You see, son? That's why I wifed your mother. She's always been TTG—shoot first, and don't ask any questions later. But she couldn't be loyal to her husband while he was behind bars."

I laughed when he said that. "Loyal? You want to talk about loyalty? How about the fact that every time you went to Miami, you were there with your mistress? Or how about how you set up shop down there and didn't let me know nothing about it?"

"So you let everything we worked hard for go because of a bitch I fucked from time to time? I never gave a fuck about that bitch, and you know that."

"No, I got rid of your ass because you wasn't shit when I met you. You must've forgotten that I put you on and showed you the ins and outs. I took you from selling dime bags of weed to copping bricks of cocaine. I taught you everything you know. All you ever cared about was making a name for yourself. You've always been a two-headed snake that would cut and kill his way to the top. Look at what you did to your own son. What real man would want to fuck his kid's life up? I'll tell you—a bitch-ass nigga who only cares about one thing, and that's becoming a kingpin. Here's a news flash: my son is the kingpin of Chicago. He did what you could never do, and that's take over these streets without the help of a woman." I paused to laugh at him.

"The Grim Reaper, huh? Bullshit. I had more heart than your bitch ass ever had. They might as well say that I was the queenpin behind the scenes, because we know that your bitch ass couldn't have done it alone. And I'm sure that just like before, you have a bitch helping you now." I laughed even harder at him. I'd waited twenty years to tell him everything I'd been holding in, and the look on his face made it obvious that he wanted to body bag me on the spot.

The whole room went quiet as he stared me down. I heard my front door open and close. Everyone in the room pulled their guns out and pointed them toward the hallway. I never took my gun or my eyes off of my ex-husband. I wanted him to give me a reason to end his life in my living room.

"Put the guns down, my sister," Porsha said as she walked into the living room wearing all black. The look on my ex-husband's face when he saw my sister was priceless. He knew that if Porsha was there, shit was going to go left. Everyone in the room look shocked—they knew of my sister but had never seen her in the flesh.

Chapter Twenty

(Malik)
From Bad Too Ugly

When I'd gotten to my mother's house, the last thing I'd been expecting to hear was this bullshit she was telling me. My whole life, I'd hated and resented my father because I'd thought that he'd left my mother to raise us alone, when in all reality, she had been lying to us the whole time. And there we were, in a room with our guns out. I could only imagine what Cinnamon was thinking. The last thing I wanted was for my girl to be caught up in this bullshit while she was pregnant with my seed. Not to mention the fact that my auntie Porsha had just walked through the door. Since she was there, I knew for a fact that shit was about to hit the fan. You see, I'd known that my mother had secrets. I hadn't known about her or my father, but I had known about my auntie. She's one of the best hit women alive, and she's who Dominique gets his orders to do his hits from.

"Well, if it isn't Porsha," my father said. "Long time, no see. I see you're still the same ol' Porsha from back in the day."

"Yeah, and I see you're still the same ol' bitch-ass nigga who couldn't run a block, let alone a whole city. I guess we both still the same, huh?"

Instead of replying to her, he looked over to me. "Listen up, son—well, all three of my children, listen up. I don't know what your mother's filled your heads up with, and I don't care. I'm telling you this out of love: stay the fuck out of my way, and I'll do the same. I would hate to go to war with my own blood, but I will. I lost all respect for y'all when you left me to rot in prison. Burning down your traps and taking your shipment was just to get your attention. I could have taken you out if I'd wanted to. I ran these streets long before you were old enough to wipe your own ass, let alone think that you were a kingpin. I'm here to let you know that as of now, I'm back, and I won't stop until I have everything that I lost."

I stood there for a minute, letting everything that bitch-ass nigga had said sink in. Not only was my mother a liar, but my father wasn't shit, and he was basically telling me that if I didn't shut down shop, he was going to do it for me. I let that shit play in my head over and over again. I looked over at Markese, who looked like he was ready to body bag our father. I walked over to where my father was. I wasn't no pussy, and I could read a muthafucka like a book. He was soft as fuck on the inside, and I wanted to see just how soft he really was.

"I see why my mother got rid of you, because you're a bitch-ass nigga." I laughed in his face. "Take a look around. I'm the king of Chicago, and I didn't need my mother's help to do it. You might as well kill me now, because I'm not going to stop shit." When I said that, Choppa, Zilla, Dominique, and Markese all walked a little closer to me. "This is my city, and I'm not going to let some bitch-ass nigga who goes by the name Grim Reaper take the shit I worked for. As a matter of fact,"—I looked around the room at my niggas— "have y'all ever heard of a nigga by the name of Grim Reaper?" I asked.

They all laughed, and Markese said, "Nah, fam. This is my first time hearing of this bitch-ass nigga." When Markese said that, he gave him a little smirk.

"Yeah, that's what I thought too. You see, you fucked up when you put money before loyalty, and a money-hungry nigga never makes it in this game," I told him.

"And a nigga with a lot to lose never makes it either. You know why, my boy? Because he's never willing to take a chance for fear of losing everything," he said with a smile on his face. "You see, I lost everything when I went into prison. The difference between you and me is that you're always going to think twice before you make a move—and me? Well, let's just say that I move without thinking—without fear of losing shit. I'll be seeing you around," he said, and then he looked over to my mother. "Till death do us part," he said, and he blew her a kiss before turning around and walking toward the front door with everyone in the room on his heels.

Once he was gone, shit hit the fan. "What the fuck just happened? Markese yelled while pacing back and forth. "How the fuck are we at war with our father? This shit never would've happened if you'd just kept it real," he said, looking over at our mother.

"I know you're mad, but you will not speak to me like that. I'm still your mother."

"Are you? You lied about everything else. Shit, you could be lying about that too." Before I knew it, she'd walked across the room and slapped fire of off my brother.

"Now, I have made some mistakes, but what the fuck you won't do is sit here and judge me. I won't let you disrespect me in my house. Who the fuck do you think you are, Markese? Huh? You big and bad? Well, let me tell your punk ass something. Way before you knew what a gun or the streets were, I was running shit. I was doing this shit way before you realized that you had balls, and you know what? Mine still are and always will be bigger than yours. You got life fucked up. You muthafuckas disrespect me or act like I'm not your mother one more time, and watch what will happen. You'll get more than a slap to the face—understand that. Now, I have a plan that will work. Y'all just have to trust me."

"I don't need or want your help," I said. "And trust you? I don't trust you or your husband," I said. I could tell that my words had cut my mother deep just by looking at her face. She was hurt, but fuck that—I was hurt too. She shouldn't have lied to me about shit, but she had, and her reason for doing it wasn't good enough for me. "Fuck all that bullshit she's saying," I thought.

"Y'all niggas can stay here and listen to what she has to say, but I'm out. Cinnamon, let's go—now!" I gave my mother one last look before I walked out of the living room. She had tears in her eyes. "Fuck those crocodile-ass tears," I thought to myself as I walked out the door with Cinnamon. What happened next was unexpected. As we walked out the front door and down the driveway, I saw men in all black jump out of a van, and then there were flashes as machine guns went off, and bullets went everywhere. I pushed Cinnamon to the ground and grabbed my strap out of my waistband. I started to shoot back. I didn't look back, but I heard a chopper going off behind me, so I knew that Choppa was there.

Markese ran up beside me and laid down two niggas dressed in all black with masks on their faces. I never even saw my auntie come out of the house, but she was behind a car giving niggas head shots like the pro she was. We were outnumbered, but we were laying muthafuckas down left and right. My mother was even out there with a TEC-9 and was letting that muthafucka spray like it was nothing. After about ten minutes of shooting it out, I heard the van start to burn rubber and pull away. I looked around my mother's front yard. There must have been at least ten dead bodies lying out there. And then it dawned on me that I didn't hear Cinnamon's voice. When I looked over to where I'd pushed her down, I saw that her body wasn't moving. I began to panic as I ran over to her.

Chapter Twenty-One

(Cinnamon)
Beginning and the End

As I sat in the living room next to Chyna and Mariah, all I could do was pray to God that he would allow everyone to walk out of the house alive. Everybody in the room had their guns out—even Malik's mother. I couldn't believe that I was caught in the middle of this bullshit—not to mention the fact that I didn't have a gun. I hadn't ever shot one before, but I wouldn't have hesitated if I had to shoot one. I'd be damned if I lost my life—or my child's life, at that. I knew that this wouldn't be the end of the war between Malik and his father, and I knew that there'd be more hell to pay because of the lies his mother had told. I could understand why she'd done what she had. I couldn't say that I would've done the same thing, but I could see where she was coming from, and I felt that Markese and Malik were being too hard on her.

I snapped out of my thoughts when Malik told me to get up so that we could go. With all of the bullshit that was going on, the last thing I was going to do was put up a fight. I couldn't help but feel like something was getting ready to happen. As I walked to the door, I felt like God was telling me not to go outside, but it was too late. As soon as we stepped foot off of the porch, all I could hear was gunfire. I was in so much of a shock that I didn't know what to do—my body froze up for the first time in my life. Before I knew it, Malik had pushed me with so much force that I flew to the ground. The last thing I saw was Choppa flying out of the house, holding two choppers in his hands and shooting at the men in all black.

I had so much pain hit me in my stomach that I knew that something had to be wrong with my baby. As I lay on the ground in pain, waiting for the gunfire to stop, all I could think of was my child, who I knew I was about to lose in a miscarriage. I felt so much pressure and had such bad cramps that all I could do was ball up until it was over. I lay there until I heard everything stop, and then Malik called my name. I didn't move or reply. I felt blood run down my leg, and I heard Chyna and Mariah yelling and crying as Malik knelt down to pick me up. He checked to see if I'd been shot, and for the first time, I realized that my shoulder and my arm were on fire. I'd been so focused on my baby that I hadn't realized that I'd been shot in the shoulder or that my arm was bleeding everywhere. The pain from the bullet caused me to start losing my vision. The more pain I felt and the more blood I lost, the heavier my eyes became. All I could hear was Malik telling me how sorry he was and saying that he loved me. I even heard Mariah on the phone crying and yelling about how she needed paramedics. I could hear Dominique and Markese going off, and before I knew it, my eyes were completely shut, and their voices began to fade away more and more until I could no longer see or hear.

To be continued.

Made in the USA
Columbia, SC
22 June 2021